BODY OF WORK

Celebrating
30 Years of Publishing
in India

Other books in the series

A Brutal Hand
Insomnia
Evoked

RAVI SUBRAMANIAN

PRESENTS

BODY OF WORK

MORTALITY IS THE ULTIMATE ART

MANSI BABBAR

HarperCollins *Publishers* India

First published in 2021

This edition published in India by HarperCollins *Publishers* in 2023
4th Floor, Tower A, Building No. 10, DLF Cyber City,
DLF Phase II, Gurugram, Haryana – 122002
www.harpercollins.co.in

2 4 6 8 10 9 7 5 3 1

P-ISBN: 978-93-5629-704-3
E-ISBN: 978-93-5629-706-7

Typeset by R. Ajith Kumar

Printed and bound at
Replika Press Pvt. Ltd.

MIX
Paper from responsible sources
FSC® C016779

This book is produced from independently certified FSC® paper to ensure responsible forest management.

'The truth is rarely pure and never simple.'

– Oscar Wilde, *The Importance of Being Earnest*

'Stupid! There were no things with claws, all hairy and full of killing spite.'

– Stephen King, *It*

CONTENTS

NOTE ON RAVI SUBRAMANIAN PRESENTS

For my readers who love pace, I offer *Ravi Subramanian Presents*. I've conceptualized these books as a series of short, plot-oriented, fast-paced novellas that are the book equivalent of caffeine for an exhausted mind. These are thrillers on steroids. There isn't a slow moment in these books, not a sentence that does not take the story forward, not a page that doesn't beg to be turned. Airports, railway stations, flights, buses, metros, bedrooms or even behind your laptops—you'd want to read your own copy of these books everywhere. These stories promise to hold you firmly in their grip until you reach the very end.

Ravi Subramanian Presents serves another purpose. I noticed that in our country, mythology and romance are popular genres and draw many capable writers. Crime writing is often considered too complicated and has not seen many writers emerge. My co-authors in this series are all brilliant writers, hand-picked by me to fill this gap. Each thriller in this series is written by a talented author with a definite flair for crime writing. It has been a pleasure to work with them and to be able to provide a platform for them.

With short, fast-paced, pulse pounding, high impact, no flab stories, *Ravi Subramanian Presents* come with a built-in accelerator. So fasten your seatbelts and get ready for the ride!

Ravi Subramanian

PROLOGUE

The distant buzz of voices stirred her awake. She fluttered her eyelids, dazed and confused. Cobwebs stuck to her arms. She felt the spindly legs of a dozen spiders making their way around her goosebumps. Before a shriek could escape her mouth, she bit her lips, just like she had with her father. A ferrous tang in her mouth made her nauseous, but she had to stay silent like a corpse.

The floor she lay on was cracked, and her back was wrung in pain. The dryness in her throat made her want to cough, but she controlled herself. A door opened with a sharp creak and she heard her attacker limp down wooden stairs, dragging something heavy, grunting in pain.

Thud ... thud ... thud ...

At each step, she heard a dull, ominous thud. Another door opened a few steps away from her; she could tell as bright yellow lights flooded her eyelids. If it weren't for her long hair, interwoven with sticky cobwebs covering her face, she'd be caught. The rain outside seemed to have stopped.

'Ready?' growled the man.

'Yes … she will be next, I assume?'

'Yeah …' He growled again and, suddenly, broke into a weird laughter like a hyena's chuckle. 'I'll take my sweet time to work on her!'

The man's snickering grew uncontrollable, and yet, he managed to pull with one hand and a limp. Sweat covered her skin, every pore crying in fear, and her heartbeat ran like the racehorse she'd seen win that morning. Every cell in her body screamed, begging her to get up and run far away from the cursed estate.

How she wished she had made the right choice when she had the time …

GLITTERBUG'S WOE

Golden letters imprinted on a matte cream-coloured invitation card glimmered under the morning sunlight on a glass-top desk. It had slipped out of an envelope that lay askew inches away on one side as if someone had slapped the desk with it angrily. The card basked in the sunlight, unaware of the storm it had invited.

'I'll ask you once again. Why did you hide this from me?' asked the short man with a disproportionately large middle. His beady eyes were squinting hard, and his dark smoker's lips were pursed into a thin line. The man's pate shone in a furious sweat, his olive skin blotched with red. If a doctor took his blood pressure, he'd call an ambulance right away, no doubt.

The only person who could make him so mad sat calmly across the table; a tall, slender woman. She had a beautiful face—her eyes were large and brown, her hair a soft touch of gold over chocolate, and her lips pink like a fresh rosebud. These features that made her face look like it should be on the cover of *Vogue* did nothing to soften the stubbornness on it. She sat with her dainty hands over her stomach, her fingers intertwined, and her legs crossed tightly.

'Why do I have to explain myself to you again?' she said softly, but firmly, looking into the old man's piercing eyes behind the glasses. He sometimes reminded her of an otter. 'I do not support that woman. I am against what she does. She ought to be punished for her sins, but our community of celebrity journalists put her on a pedestal instead, while the law is handicapped in front of her money and power. I will not go even if she begs me to come.'

'That woman you speak of,'—the old man's eyes bulged in anger, and he leaned over the table on his elbows, resembling an otter a little more as his wispy moustache twitched—'is an international artist who owns a production house, a music label, has award-winning movies to her name, runs a charity for single and widowed mothers, and is a diva even in her fifties. She's a legend in the Indian film industry and a star in Hollywood. She's—'

'A prostitute, who encourages nepotism, casting couch and underhand methods to get top ratings.'

'What underhand methods get you box office hits in ten countries? It doesn't work that way,' the man countered, but she ignored him.

'She has captured hundreds of acres for her real estate project *illegally*. Praise her a thousand times if you like, but I won't ever listen. That woman is not right.'

'You are refusing to see objectively. Keep your bias aside, Raina!'

'There is no bias, Vin,' Raina said and shoved her elbow almost through the table, mimicking Vin. 'She misuses her fame. You know it. Ever since she rose to stardom thirty years ago, supported by that filthy director, she's been on a magical winning spree! There's a lot of evidence of all the dodgy things she's done to ensure her spree doesn't end—'

'Where's the evidence?' Vin spat, a fat droplet traversing from his mouth to her side. Raina's nose flared in anger and disgust.

'Why isn't there a single report against her? It's all social chatter and losers' rants,' Vin said.

'It's obvious she takes care of that with dirty tricks!' Her fists curled.

'Raina, I know you've been through a lot, but accusing anyone without evidence—especially an international celebrity—is slandering and defaming! As a celebrity reporter of *Glitterbug* magazine, as a journalist reporting to me, the least you could do is stop being so reckless!' His pitch rose as he uttered the word 'reckless'.

'I'm not reckless!'

'Then what would you call it? There's a bunch of them doing illegal things. Are you going to expose them all? What is this—*Pokémon*? Gotta catch 'em all?' He gestured dramatically with his free arm. Raina stared at him, wanting to scream.

'You are being ridiculous!' said Raina. 'I am not interested in everyone, because not everyone is as rotten as her, and I'll prove it to you one day, maybe today! I'll waltz into her stupid launch party as you say and get you some hard evidence. Remember, you asked for it!'

'Give it a try! One more stunt like this and I'll fire you. This is my limit,' he said, jabbing the cream card. 'You've already put me in a spot by going against her. Do it once more, and you'll be the sacrificial goat. Either make up with her and keep this job, or give your career up. This is really the last chance, Raina!'

'It was not baseless! I had the evidence but you all ignored it!'

'Drunken testimonies are no evidence!'

'And why do you think she has invited me knowing that I accused her?' Raina said, as she grabbed the envelope and waved it in front of his face. 'It's a VIP event with a handful of media personnel. Why me? I'm her arch-enemy.'

'I don't know!' Vin shrugged impatiently. 'Maybe she wants to give you a chance instead of suing you? I don't care why. Stars are whimsical. Who knows what they're thinking. But it's a big opportunity for *Glitterbug*! Stop being a pain and do your job, for God's sake! You are a Bollywood reporter, not a crime investigator.'

Raina's jaws clenched and her eyes darkened. Vin had touched a nerve with that last sentence. Her breathing became shorter and sharper. Vin's face softened a degree watching her face become stony. He had no clue, but Bollywood reporting was never what Raina wanted to do. She had always wanted to bring the truth out as a journalist, as a crime reporter, but life had dealt her the shorter end of the stick. How she wished she could hurl a punch at Vin and quit this silly job.

'Raina,' his voice dropped to a calmer tone, 'I had removed you from her account; I'd have kept it that way too, but *you* got this invitation. It's the launch of the most expensive residential project in India. People from all over want in, but only a few can go! We are very lucky! *Glitterbug* needs more sales to survive after your disaster.

'I'm only asking you to do your job as a journalist. Look, observe and report what you see. We're barely surviving as it is, so please be smart about it.'

Raina didn't say a word. It burned her insides when Vin reminded her how to do her job, but what could she say?

She was caught between a rock and a hard place now that the invite had been found lying in her bin. A job, a source of income, was necessary for her. Being an orphan, she had no one to support her. Going to this launch party, however, would be slaughtering of her values as a journalist. Vin's eyes were losing their temporary softness to her cold silence.

'If you don't go, you'll not only get on her bad side again but mine too. You either report the event or leave this job.' Vin leaned back into his puffy leather chair. It made a weird noise as his weight shifted. On another time and day, Raina would have snorted with derision.

'This is blackmail,' she said, her teeth clenched.

'The invitation is personally addressed to you and your team,' he said with a casual shrug. 'I can't change the name on the card.'

Raina couldn't understand why she had been chosen for this dubious honour. She looked at the card. Her name glimmered in gold, and as the sun's rays streamed in through the window, she could see Infiniti Mall, Andheri West, not too far away. Even as the traffic made a din out on the road between the office and the mall, everything went blank for Raina. She couldn't hear anything but her heartbeat—an irregular, uneasy heartbeat. Was it her hatred—for the situation, for the person—she wondered, that made her want to go straight home and lock herself in her room?

Whatever it was, it would have to quieten down, for the need for survival in the world trumped everything else.

'Raina,' Vin called out with a raised brow. 'I've always allowed you freedom at work. You have been great for the last three years, and I know you can do well in life if you stop going after the wrong people.' His brows rose higher, almost to his non-existent hairline. Raina sighed in resignation.

'Fine ... now that you have your finger on my jugular, I'll do it,' she said coldly and stood up, grabbing the invitation card. 'I'll look, observe, and report objectively. If I find anything to worry about, I'll report that too. Fire me if you can after I get you evidence.'

'If *Glitterbug* is harmed in any way, let me warn you again, we're done. You won't get a job anywhere in the media industry if you play this wrong, you know that, right?'

'We'll see,' said Raina, bold but covered in goosebumps, as she stared into Vin's cold, beady eyes. She turned sharply, her hair bouncing about her shoulders, and left. Vin sighed and gulped a glass of water.

'She's sucking the life out of me,' he sighed and leaned further back into his chair.

Raina threw the invite on her table, much like Vin had after he found the card in her garbage bin that morning. She sighed, cursing her fate, and dumped herself on her chair. Her dress, a grey one-piece with a boat neck, felt hot after the whole conversation.

'I don't understand …' Raina's colleague came riding on her revolving chair closer to her desk as she bit on an apple, '… why do you hate Hera so much? True, she started with her daddy's support and rose to fame after—as you say—selling herself, but after that, she's been doing well on her own. Is it her privilege you hate or her wealth?'

'I hate the fact that she misuses her privilege and wealth. There's no fair play with her presence in the industry! Everyone knows you can't be cast in a movie, TV series or commercial, or even a modelling show if she's involved and her favours are not given when asked for. And guess what? She's almost always involved.' Raina put her neck against the backrest, still frowning.

'The bitch has her hands everywhere! Remember Vanya, the playback singer for Hera's movie? How she was stripped by the media and shamed? Controversy after controversy trailed her, so much so that the girl broke down in a press conference and had to hide for months. Word is that Vanya refused some favour for Hera. There's not a single person involved with her even remotely who escaped scratch-free!'

'Hmm … but how can you say she was behind Vanya's ill-fate?'

'It's the pattern of every person who's under her rule. And, well, people talk when they are drunk. All you need to do is listen.'

'And record.'

'Yeah, well, but that's not *credible*.' Raina held her hands up to make air quotes as she uttered the word 'credible'. 'I have plenty of drunken testimonies … but if the police investigate—if they dare to step up—these recordings would become the so-called inadmissible statements … I need something more solid.'

'More solid?' The girl stared at Raina in disbelief, 'You haven't given up on it at all, have you?'

Raina held her obvious answer back. Vin's words boomed in her mind. She couldn't defame *Glitterbug* and risk getting fired. She needed this job; if she wanted to keep it, she'd have to swallow indignation. Once she lands legal proof, she can enter the world of real crime reporting, be free to expose the so-called celebrities. At the very thought of that possibility, her blood gushed and she smiled, rocking back and forth in her chair. The uneasiness in her heart was shrouded in adrenaline.

Six months ago, Raina had dated an assistant director in Hera Productions Pvt. Ltd who had interacted with Hera many times.

'Hera? Who the fuck is Hera? It's Antara Malik! Mrs Antara Dev Malik on her passport, that sneaky bitch ... Do you know what she said to me today?'

'What?' Raina blinked, already high after smoking several blunts.

'She said I should entertain her if she was to entertain me as a first assistant director in her production house ... I said I have a girlfriend and she laughed it off. Handed me her running shoes and asked me to give them to her butler ... that bloody old man ... When I did, he asked me to hand over my ID card and leave. I lost my job in a minute. A minute! What's it to her? Nothing!' He waved an arm and let it fall beside him.

'What now?' Raina asked.

'Nothing ... I'll return to my dad's office and run the business. Being a simple cloth merchant in a small town is better than selling my soul to the devils in this place ... can't lick 'em there to keep a job.'

'You are lucky. At least you have a way out ... you don't have to keep lickin' em there ...'

'Yeah, sorry that we'll have to split. I cannot ruin my life here.'

She never saw him after that day. There was no message or call after the ten-odd dates she'd had with him. But then, she got shocking news. A local news channel reported his death. They said he was into drugs and had overdosed in his apartment. In the six months she had known him and another month she had dated him, he had never taken drugs. He had decided to return home for a better life; it made no sense he could overdose. Raina had been dating him casually, but she felt she had to investigate

The Hera Productions office was close to that of *Glitterbug*, and the crew usually chose bars in the area to drown their exertions in alcohol, nicotine and marijuana. She'd go alone, wait for them to get drunk, and move closer to place her recorders in the couch gaps. Once the alcohol loosened their tongues, people needed just a nudge to start talking. A nudge like 'Dude, you look like a zombie from hell!' had the best effect. Raina had soon recorded more than a hundred people talking about how Hera exploited actors, singers, new crew members and basically anyone she could. They spoke about her fearsome grip on everyone around, the power of connections and reach in the political circles. No one could squeak without her knowing, they said. No one could move without her wish.

'She's like Sauron. Her ever-watchful eye is on us all,' said a guy and hiccuped. His hands shook after three straight days of shooting and a tubful of alcohol. He was on the verge of a breakdown. 'If I dare show my face, make her notice me in any way, I'll be done for like our brother here.' He pointed an oscillating finger at another man.

'I ... I don't think I can take it anymore. Wanting things to be perfect is one thing, but it's impossible to work under so much pressure.'

'Why is she treating you this way, though?' Raina asked the crew members, pretending to be high.

'She saw me shirtless one day. I was setting up cameras all over on a beach in Goa—it was our location for a music video—and since then, she wants me to take up a night job in some high-end strip club. She said she will be my only client, and all I have to do is model for her whenever she wants.'

'What? That sounds like she wants you to be her gigolo.'

'Damn ... I said I couldn't do it. My career, my dream is cinematography!'

'Just do the favour, you guys, and lead a good life!' said a girl sitting at the end of the group. She was wearing shorts and a neon pink bralet with a chiffon shrug over it. 'It's a matter of as long as you work for her.'

'Yeah, well, easy for you to say! Your favour was simply to dress in these clothes. And I highly doubt her favours are temporary. There is hardly any place where she doesn't have influence.'

'You never know. Some people get off easy. You remember that guy who was begging for a chance to audition after the deadline had passed? She asked him to dance for her and showcase his skills. In private.' The girl shrugged.

'This is draining the life out of me ...' The guy buried his head in his arms.

'Why don't you involve lawyers or police?' asked Raina.

They chuckled, looking at each other and shaking their heads.

'Babe,' the girl looked at Raina, putting her beer down, 'you cannot win a case against her. The police will beat us up if we try anything. It has happened to our colleagues who wanted justice.'

'There is no justice in show business.'

'Oh, come on, it's just one fish stinking up the pond ...'

As the three crew members began debating if it was one crazy woman ruining the industry or was the industry friendly to people like her, Raina shifted her thoughts on finding more proof.

As Raina continued her research, she came across hushed news, small paragraphs in news online, and some local news articles in Marathi about how Hera's real estate business was causing farmers to protest. Further north, on the outskirts of Mumbai, Hera had spearheaded a large project spread across two hundred acres of land. Agricultural land, as well as residential sites of other builders, had been bought. Farmers alleged they were being forced out. Builders reserved their comments.

With some more research, she could put together the

pieces of Hera Realty & Construction being responsible for the expansion of office buildings and shopping areas against the local protests and on dodgy permissions. While farmers had lost acreage in rural areas beyond Borivali, many civilians had to give up their expensive square feet. Glaring questions about the buyout related to the latest launch of Golden Hera Farmhouses were hushed. With so much evidence of apparent wrongdoings, Raina couldn't but slip an article in *Glitterbug* about Hera's black business.

They did not get any rebuttal on the article from Hera's media and realty companies, but *Glitterbug* was attacked by a million people for the allegations. Many news channels, news dailies and magazines made *Glitterbug* a laughing stock and took the opportunity to, as Raina called it, 'ass-lick' Hera. Social media buzzed with extreme hate against Raina as well. Hera had a loyal following and equally loyal social media managers.

Thinking about it all was making her head ache. As Raina went back to her small, one-room apartment to change into a dress appropriate for a big event, she felt no guilt for the losses *Glitterbug* had to face the last quarter. She picked up her denims, a formal top and a blazer, matching them with black boots fit for a rough day in a farmhouse. The uneasiness in her heart had still not vanished; instead, it churned the painful feeling of acid in her gut, making her feel bitter. The adrenaline was gone, and powerlessness stung.

If only she had made a better choice years ago, when she could have chosen the right path in her life, she wouldn't be working for Glitterbug *at all* ...

She watched her reflection in the mirror and sighed. Her phone buzzed. The name 'Ronit' flashed on the screen. Smiling, Raina swiped right to answer the call on speaker as she put her make-up on.

'Ready?' she asked excitedly. Ronit was the reason her days at *Glitterbug* were passable. It didn't hurt that he looked great and seemed to like her.

'Ronnie is always ready for you! Why don't you come into my arms in another minute?'

'Stop it!' She smiled. 'I'm glad you are picking me up. It can pour like the end of the Earth anytime now that it's mid-June and we are going to a damn farmhouse.'

'No worries! You have me. I bet today's going to be very interesting. Feels kind of like a date, just you and me—'

'—And hundreds of others!' Raina zipped her bag, as she held the phone between her ear and a shoulder. 'I'm all packed. Be down in a minute.'

She smiled and hung up. Ronit had been asking her out for months now, after the boyfriend from Hera Productions had disappeared, and she got labelled as *Glitterbug*'s woe. He had liked her for a long time, he had confessed, but Raina needed more time. He was a handsome man with the wit and intelligence of a prince charming, and he was good at what he did. Raina felt she had to do better to be with him. She wasn't enough, not just yet, being a mocked celebrity journalist. If there was another reason for her to become a sought-after crime reporter, besides wanting that for herself, it was to be able to say yes to Ronit without feeling small.

A few minutes later she was downstairs and saw his white Creta standing at a distance. A wave of warmth filled Raina when he turned to her with his dark, curling hair falling just above his warm, chicory brown eyes. He smiled, soft dimples embellishing his cheeks. She ran towards him with a puppy enthusiasm.

'At your service, ma'am!'

'Well, thanks!' she said, smiling, as she got into the car and gave him a quick hug. 'Thank God I don't have to do this alone.' The road ahead was long, roughly a three-hour drive. They'd arrive barely at lunchtime. Ronit had arranged a playlist for the drive and had stored snacks in the backseat. Raina put aside heavy thoughts and enjoyed the drive beside him. How she wished things could be as simple as this drive every day. The bright golden sun and good music—it could have been her life if only she'd made a different choice all those years ago.

THE HANDICAPPER

The day was at its brightest as the two sped through a pothole-free road—a rare occurrence in Mumbai—and entered a distinct green region dotted with farms beyond Virar. Huge boards and arches over the road indicated they were two kilometres away from the Golden Hera farmhouses.

'I can't believe this road could've been so smooth before,' Raina remarked. She had rolled the window down and was looking at the broad, clean road with footpaths and cycle tracks. There were guard posts every five hundred metres.

'I don't think there ever was a road here at all!' said Ronit as he stopped at a guard post. He held up the invitation and their identities. The guard in a crisp navy uniform gestured to his colleague to open the automatic wedge barrier. The iron wedge recessed, and Ronit drove on.

'That's some serious security ...' said Raina.

'People getting houses here won't need to cross them, though.'

'Why?'

'They all have personal helipads.' Ronit glanced at her with a smirk. Raina scoffed, shaking her head.

'Such entitled people ...'

'For today, Hera is sponsoring their helicopters. Later, they can either get their own helis or rent one from Hera Hospitality Services. Only the housekeepers would need this road daily.'

Raina stared darkly at the rolling green ahead of them. Hera Hospitality Services provided all types of luxury vehicles and villas for rent and manpower for all kinds of events, including corporate parties. Raina had her doubts about what really happened behind the scene. As they drove closer, she could point out a golf course to her right, a resort to her left and a beautiful astronomical observation tower ahead of the resort. The place was a dream, untouched by the reality of commoners.

They soon reached a huge black gate flanked by boundary walls that seemed to extend forever. They had to get a pass made before entering rows between lavish, huge independent villas surrounded by gardens, swimming pools and treehouses. Raina was astounded when, on her right, she saw beautiful horses—brown, white and black—running freely in a fenced ranch.

'That's our first stop,' said Ronit, holding the invite in his hand. 'The race must be in the last leg.' He followed the map printed in gold on the back of the invite. They approached a parking point, where a valet opened their doors and took the car keys, handing Ronit a metallic coupon. They walked past the stables where jockeys adjusted reins and bridles on their horses. The groomed skins on the back of the animals shone in the noon sun. They were ready for the last round.

'My bet is on number five, Black Jack.' A husky baritone caught Raina's attention. She turned and saw a tall man steps away from her. He had a full head of grey hair, drawn into a sleek ponytail, and a well-kept white moustache and beard. The man had unusually large hands. His eyes were coal-black and small behind frameless glasses. She guessed he was about sixty. Despite the sun, the man was dressed in a white wing-collared shirt, a grey vest and a black morning coat. His black silk tie shone. In his fitted trouser and coat, he looked like a butler straight out of a movie set.

'That's Don, Hera's butler,' whispered Ronit, almost on cue.

'Are you sure, sir? Black Jack couldn't be in the top three, let alone win any of the rounds,' said the bookie. 'The horse is bad news.'

'It's the jockey who didn't win the rounds. This time he'll win big,' Don said.

'No way ... there's no bet on that one.'

'Well, I'm in for good money then,' Don said, watching the perplexed guy with an impassive look. He then pulled white cotton gloves over his hands, tucking the edges in the cuffs of his shirt, and walked away.

'He's the one who asks people to fuck off on Hera's command,' Raina said, watching the man stand tall with the confidence of a millionaire. Was that how a butler looked?

They went behind Don and reached an air-conditioned room atop the stand, where the elite few were enjoying the race with glasses of Möet & Chandon in their hands. Dainty champagne flutes tinkered as waiters, dressed spotlessly in black and white, served drinks and snacks. Ronit picked two glasses and offered one to Raina.

'I don't drink.'

'Whoa, never knew that!' Ronit exclaimed, sipping the expensive champagne.

'I do it only when it's absolutely needed.'

'Like when you need people to talk.'

'Yeah,' she chuckled tonelessly. 'Not many good memories with alcohol, that's all.'

'What, did you regret something the next day?'

'It's a long, ugly story for some other time.' She let out a sigh. Ronit didn't press on, but he wondered why the topic made her uncomfortable.

The race was exciting. Much to Raina's surprise, Don turned out to be right. Black Jack won by a huge margin, stunning everyone.

'His prediction is never wrong. How sharp a handicapper he is! I should have him join our board; we'll probably never face a loss,' a lady commented. 'The guy hasn't lost a single bet!'

The group started trickling down the stairs, directed by several attendants, towards the lunch hall. Hera's own farmhouse just behind the stands was to host the party.

'I haven't spotted her yet, have you?' Raina asked Ronit as they climbed down the stairs. He shook his head, holding a fresh refill of champagne in his hand. As they crossed the stands, she heard a dull rifle shot from far right. She looked towards the open field beside the racecourse.

'You have good ears, young lady.' Raina turned with a slight start as Don's deep voice came from behind her. She hadn't noticed him at all! 'Do you want to see the firing range? You could watch the match between our young master and Sarah.'

'Sarah?'

'She is our housekeeper,' said Don, stretching an arm courteously, bowing slightly at the waist, and gesturing her to walk towards the ranch.

Reluctant to appear rude, partly because men were not as courteous these days, she followed with Ronit in tow. She was led to the main office of the range, through which she walked towards a wide corridor facing a fenced ground. Targets stood far away, close to the fence, and participants stood with rifles. There were five people. Three, who had already lost the matches, were watching the two participants competing now—a man and a woman. Raina noticed that the woman was in a pleated black dress with white collar and a white apron over it. Raina was immediately reminded of Japanese cafe maids, though the look on her face was anything but *kawaii*. Her hair was tied in an elegant French knot. She was slender and graceful with a dusky face and sharp, cat-like green eyes. Focusing on the target made her look like a precarious predator. She stood so still one could mistake her for a statue until she made a perfect shot. People clapped, and she smiled reservedly. Her downturned full lips were painted a nude cinnamon.

A young man, not more than twenty, was smiling at Sarah as he stood a few steps away, waiting his turn. Raina didn't fail to notice he was handsome and looked familiar to her. He was in a white linen shirt, sleeves rolled up to hint at a muscular frame, and designer navy trousers with a matching vest. His hair fell over his forehead as he now took aim.

'Hera's son, Ved ...' Raina whispered to herself. She remembered him from his photo shoot in *Vogue*. He'd ventured into modelling, but had stayed away from the movies so far. Hera had said in an interview that Ved had interests other than acting. Raina wondered what those could be besides living a lavish life. He shot and groaned as he missed the bull's eye by an inch.

'You win, like always,' Ved said with a boyish shrug as he took his headgear off and clapped along with the other participants for Sarah, who bowed courteously to Ved and gestured him to lead the way outside.

'Let me escort you back towards the party, Ms Roy,' said Don. 'Lunch is already served.'

'So you know me,' Raina said.

'You are famous in this household,' he replied nonchalantly.

Raina followed the tall butler, staring at his wide shoulders. No one could say he was nearing sixty if they saw his back; the man seemed to have done some heavy lifting in the earlier decades of life. He led Raina and Ronit to a beautiful garden behind the racecourse stands, through a cobblestone path, and into a huge white mansion. A wide oak door was open to let the elite swarm buzz in and out.

Raina entered the most beautiful and open piece of real estate she'd ever seen in her life. Her jaw dropped as she set foot in a foyer with lights fitted into the ceiling. Before her was a huge hall with walls textured in tints of gold, a shining floor of polished marble and long tables laid out with decor like that of a royal wedding reception. Beyond the hall where lunch was being served was another set of open oak doors leading to a fireplace. Big, cushioned couches decorated the centre of the main hall.

'I hope you'll find the arrangements to your liking, Ms Roy,' Don said as he bowed elegantly. 'I must take your leave. There is something I have to attend to.'

'Sure, thanks ...' she replied awkwardly, unused to such hospitality, and watched him go.

'You don't have a crush on him, do you?' Ronit asked, nibbling on a triangle of Brie.

'As if! Who talks like that in today's world?' She snorted and shook her head. Don was charming, and yet, she wondered, why did a sense of fear make her skin crawl when he was in her vicinity?

'I'll be back,' said Raina and strode towards the fireplace through the sitting room. The elite swarm were gathered in there. Some talked in small groups while others stood in front of a wall appreciating something. Perhaps she could pick up something about the mysterious star who was also her host for this evening. Raina made her way around the small groups towards the point of attraction. A life-size portrait of Hera, standing beside a black horse, hung on the wall. Several other paintings surrounded the portrait: a woman in Africa, a child in a Chinese village, dancers from Barcelona, a scene from Don Quixote where Marcela addresses the funeral of Chrysostom, and, last but not least, a Greek Goddess sitting on a golden throne. The Goddess was dressed in white robes and was adorned with a gold, cylindrical crown. Each painting had a small sign at the bottom.

'You seem to like my paintings.'

Raina jerked her neck to the right. She had never met her in person, but she would recognize the enchanting, musical voice of Antara Malik anywhere. She was tall, slender and spotless. The grace with which she carried herself was exotic, instantly setting her apart from the crowd. The ivory-white gown she wore hugged her hourglass figure and complemented her light-brown eyes.

'Hera …' Raina blurted. 'Why did you invite me?'

'Straight to the point, aren't we?' She folded an arm over the other and sipped from her glass of champagne before continuing. 'What do you think of my collection here? I've made every stroke of these paintings with utmost love and care ... They will be a part of my *oeuvre*, my body of work, as an artist.'

Raina stared at the stunning beauty who stood close to her. The same creepy feeling she had felt around Don revisited her.

'I didn't know you painted.' That was all she could manage to say.

'Of course.' Hera smiled, her eyes enigmatic. 'This is a hobby. I intend to paint a lot more, add to my collection, and lease it someday to the museums, but the paintings remain a family treasure. They are very personal, you see, like this one—' She pointed a slim finger at the gilt-framed painting titled *Marcela's Tears*. 'She wanted to be free, not forced into anything, but the hypocritical and disillusioned society didn't like it. The romance, the love Chrysostom felt was but a tantrum. He jumps into a pond because she doesn't accept his advances. At his funeral, Marcela basically tells everyone to back the fuck off and let her live in peace, to open their eyes to reality. I loved that part of the book. But am I rambling on? Have you ever read *Don Quixote*?' Hera's eyes fell on Raina's face, scrutinising every pore. Raina gulped.

'No, not much of a reader ...'

'Ahh ... that explains a lot of things ...' Hera's smile turned into a half grin. 'Then you wouldn't know much about Hera, would you?'

'That I do, after researching you,' Raina gathered her wits quickly for a retort. 'A Greek goddess, one of the twelve Olympians, an extremely jealous wife and always blind in anger.'

'Sad …' Hera sighed, her eyes still on Raina. 'How quick we are to judge wives as jealous, while cheating husbands are considered powerful Gods. Do you know how many affairs and illegitimate children Zeus is supposed to have had? Or how he treated Hera?'

'Well, that gives Hera no reason to kill the mortal women, who were mostly victims themselves,' said Raina, as she picked up a glass of champagne from a passing tray. There were times other than evidence collection when alcohol helped.

'For once, I agree. She should have killed Zeus instead. He already feared her, and she had the power.' Hera took her second sip and a deep breath. She gestured to the paintings. 'The self-portrait is my best to date. I painted it without a reference picture.'

If it were any other person, Raina would have expressed amazement. Now, she simply swirled her champagne, stone-faced.

'You haven't answered me,' she said.

'The answer to your question is not that simple, but in short …' Hera's gaze held hers. A strange numbness rushed through Raina's veins, making her cold and jittery. It was those eyes with no sign of warmth. Those enigmatic eyes that evoked chaos. Was she getting nervous for no reason? 'I wanted to impress you. I hoped you could be persuaded to write me a positive review. No lies, of course. Based only on what you see and discover at this launch event.' Hera was scanning every bit of Raina's face. 'I'm only human, Ms Roy!'

'You cannot persuade me to do anything, Hera. I can do my job without anyone telling me how. I will uncover any facts that need uncovering.'

'Well, then, enjoy your exploration! I suggest you explore the farmhouse as much as you wish and let me know if you need anything ... except for what you are looking for.' Hera chuckled and turned to leave.

'Did you win at the race today?' Raina asked. Hera stopped and turned to look at her again.

'Around two-fifty thousand rupees, yes, which will now be donated to my charity.'

'Betting to raise charity money, are we now?'

'I don't see why not. That kind of money is pocket change for people here. Just imagine how much was collected today, for the needy. Surely even you could find nothing wrong with helping the less fortunate,' Hera said with a smirk before walking away, her gown trailing her. Raina's face was blotted with scarlet anger and embarrassment. If Raina had to bet on something, it would be on how Don had paid the jockeys to play to Hera's will. But no evidence, no story. And this woman's mask never slipped. There had to be something that would reveal her real face ...

CRITTERS IN FRAY

Raina watched Hera smoothly mingle with her guests. Everyone wanted a piece of her—to grab her attention, get an exclusive minute with her. Her son came in, a bunch of people forming his convoy, mostly young women with bright eyes that gave away their intention of nabbing a rich, handsome boy. He seemed to enjoy the attention as he drank and flirted with the fawning young women. Raina noticed the young woman from the afternoon, Sarah, serving the guests, bowing gracefully and offering drinks to Ved's party.

'No one compares to her from that kiddie crowd,' Ronit said as he watched Sarah go around in high heels as if doing a catwalk in them was normal for her. 'She's hot.'

'Agreed … and I thought she and Ved were friendly, but he seems to look at her only as a shooting range companion.'

Raina had found a small table in a corner with a full view of the fireside seating where the party was in full swing. She sat with Ronit, a plate of salad in front of her, as her eyes darted around, taking everything in. The champagne she had picked up earlier sat half-finished. Rohit noticed it but didn't say anything. A woman in a short yellow bodycon dress entered. Raina watched her look around frantically, straightening her dress, and force a smile on her face when she spotted Ved.

'Wait a minute! That's Vanya, the singer Hera chucked out!' Raina whispered, astounded.

'Yeah, well, I heard she was seeking therapy. Looks like it worked for her,' Ronit said with a chuckle.

Vanya walked up to Ved and greeted him. He greeted her with a distant smile, while still seated, and returned to the conversation he was having with his admirers. Vanya stood in her spot like a damaged doll, the ghost of a smile frozen on her face. After a few minutes, she walked towards the corner where Raina and Ronit sat. She stopped a few steps away, seeing an almost hidden mirror, and began to adjust her dress; she pulled her dress down and pushed the sides of her breasts together for a deeper cleavage. Raina blinked in disbelief as she saw her retouch her make-up, fix her smile, and go back to Ved. This time when she bent to talk to him, he paid attention and offered her a seat.

'I thought she'd press charges! I guess now we know why she didn't,' Raina said, clearly upset.

'No proof that Hera did anything,' Ronit said and shrugged. 'She alleged that Hera paid the media to write shit about her. Ruined her career and so on. But where's the evidence? Raina,'—he pulled his chair closer to her—'why don't you see it's all in your head? Employees talk shit and even lie about their bosses, especially when emboldened by a drink or two. It happens, and in this industry, it happens a lot. These people hug each other with smiles on their faces and knives in their hands! You can't possibly believe all that you hear in bars!' He looked at her, brows raised.

Raina opened her mouth to retort but fell silent. Could Ronit be right? Was this just how showbiz was run? People talked shit, and she had been misled into believing Hera abused her power? But then, what about the reports she had got from local sources about farmers being forcefully evicted from the very land she was rubbing her nervous toes on? How could there be smoke if there was no fire? She had tried to find out more about this land before Hera took ownership of it, but had found no leads for comments or to support the small news articles. Even the newspapers that published the articles had refused to comment.

Ved said something to Vanya, and she got up. She walked towards the hall where lunch was laid out. Raina stood up and followed her. She saw Vanya stop at the main course section and start plating lunch. Amidst the noise of cutlery and soft classical music playing from soundbars, Raina inched closer to Vanya. She picked up a ceramic plate and stood close to Vanya, picking up a ladle and serving whatever was nearest. The smile on Vanya's face was now an expression of apprehension; her hands fumbled as they served the Chinese main course onto the plate she held. Every serving she picked from the containers, she placed carefully on the plate, as if she was making a work of art.

'You are serving lunch for her son after what she did to you?'

Vanya flinched on hearing Raina's voice.

'You almost made me drop this!' she said plaintively, but almost immediately, her tone changed. 'I know you. Stop snooping around,' she hissed.

'Oh, snooping around, is it?' Raina glared at her. 'Didn't you approach me first with your story of *alleged* victimisation by the mighty Hera?'

'I was wrong, okay?' Vanya's face paled. She gulped. 'I overreacted. Please, I need to make this right and thank her properly for letting me have another chance—'

'What did she make you do in exchange for that chance? Is showing skin a part of the deal?'

Vanya turned away, almost shaking at the fact that someone might spot her with the nosy reporter.

'Stop asking these questions. Stop investigating Hera. You will not get anything. No one gains from doing what you are trying to do,' she said and walked away, leaving Raina stunned into silence. She watched Vanya stride out of the hall and back to Ved. Her watery smile was back on as she offered Ved the plate of food. He looked at her, said something, and turned away towards another woman. Vanya stood holding the plate, standing aside like a serf. Nevertheless, she smiled bravely and took a seat nearby.

'I have known Hera for two decades now,' said a woman attired in a gaudy magenta anarkali, embroidered all over with golden thread. Her clothes made Raina wish she had brought her aviators.

'I was always a supporter, a proud supporter!' the woman said, her double chin wobbling in pride.

'Incredible! You must have seen her through it all; the start of her career and her subsequent success.'

'Yes, in fact, I knew her father as well. He was the one who got her her first contract with Balram Dixit, God bless his soul, and she got five movies with him in three short years! After that, her father passed away,' she said solemnly as she gulped her pina colada.

'You must have been a great support to her in those times ...' Raina nodded in fake concern.

'Of course I was, but,'—she hiccuped softly and her eyes were red with a bit too much drink—'between us, he wasn't the best of dads. He had forced her to sign a three-year contract with Dixit, who was just the worst. I'm so happy she charted her own path in modelling and music videos. That led her to Hollywood, as we all know. And from there on, she was unstoppable!'

'Yeah, only till she married.'

'Ahh ...' the lady clicked her tongue. 'Her husband ... Abhiram Malik was just a hollow of a man. If he hadn't been rich, he'd be nothing. The first year of their marriage was wonderful, but then he ... ' her voice trailed off, as if suddenly conscious of how much she had gossiped. 'Oh, well, personal matters must remain just so. I'm goddamn drunk, aren't I?'

'Of course, of course. I'm just glad she had you with her in those tough times. I kind of know what had happened back then with ... you know ...' Raina raised her eyebrows knowingly, baiting the older woman to complete her unfinished sentence. The woman took the bait easily.

'So you know about his affairs. Well,' she said, as she shrugged her flabby shoulders and shook her head, 'he couldn't keep it in his pants. Just like he couldn't stop the drinking. I'm sure there's more to it than just affairs, though I never dared to ask.'

'Why? You are her confidante! She would definitely tell you.' Raina frowned in wonderment, nudging the woman to say more.

'I think he might have been into drugs because of the way he died, but you never know. The post-mortem report didn't show anything but an unfortunate cardiac arrest. It was dead of the night when they say he died. Ved was still a baby, and she was sleeping with him. Abhiram was in his home office.' She shook her head and sighed.

'How sad, they were under the same roof and yet, Hera couldn't save him in time,' Raina said. Another bet she'd place would be that Hera planned her husband's death. After all, Hera should have killed Zeus instead of tolerating his nonsense, and got herself freedom like Marcela.

'I'm so glad Donnie joined soon after,' the woman continued. 'He looked after her and the household after this tragedy. He saw that Ved never felt lonely when she couldn't be there for him.'

'Ahh, right. He's a thorough gentleman.'

'Just imagine what a shock it would've been to the boy. The poor little boy,' she said, gulping down some more pina colada.

'Indeed,' Raina muttered. She decided to take the conversation into slightly risky territory. 'It is still weird the way he died, isn't it? He seemed fit. I mean, he was into horse-riding, golf and soccer.'

'The way he drank, though, it was a matter of when, not if. Hera suffered a lot in her marriage, and I am the witness. She did whatever it took to achieve a standing in this world, and I respect her for that.'

'Whatever it took, like what? No one in news talks about what one does to get to the top—' Raina asked, blinking innocuously.

Suddenly the woman looked into her eyes, her lips pursed shut and her gaze dark. The drunken glee was gone.

'Listen, girl, all you need to understand is that Hera is the greatest woman of all times,' the woman cut in. 'She achieved what she has today by working her way up. Her father did nothing for her, contrary to what y'all believe. And she is an astute businesswoman. So, I recommend you focus on the facts and write that down next time instead of looking for a controversy.'

'Why would I look for controversy where there is none?' Raina said, dropping her act. 'I'm here at this party because I am looking for facts.'

The woman's red eyes were unfocused as she narrowed them.

'Brace yourself for a storm because that's what you are looking for,' she said as she finished the pina colada in a loud gulp and slammed down the glass on a table beside them. 'Everyone here knows who you are. Whatever you're planning to uncover, it's useless,' she said and, as if her aggression was a momentary illusion, smiled gleefully again. 'I suggest you look around and support Hera's efforts in making the world better!' She stood up, patted Raina's shoulder and walked away. Raina stayed still, dazed. Clearly, the woman had been playing her. All the guests knew who she was, and they were on their guard. Her investigation had been doomed from the beginning.

Ronit was already through three rounds of the main course before he decided to get to work and record the event. By the time Raina shook herself out of her disturbed daze, Ronit was filming. She got on with her job, switching to her celebrity journalist avatar, describing the launch party, the events, asking questions to the celebrities gathered under Hera's roof about what they were wearing for the event. Many of them shared their delight in being associated with the star's venture; others glorified her already exalted status. It was as if Raina had entered the world of sixteenth-century Parisian courts where merchants had to put their best face on to please the king. They were merely critters, in muddy waters fretting for survival.

Suddenly the grandeur of the place—the silk tablecloths, sparkling cutlery, tasteful furniture, lace curtains, gleaming marble floors and crystal knickknacks—all seemed to be the skin of a hideous monster.

The lunch was followed by a tour of another ready-for-sale mansion next to Hera's. There were violinists, cellists and pianists in the halls and gardens of the tour property reproducing compositions of Bach, Beethoven and Chopin. Raina felt as if their music was perfume attempting to cover up the rotten smell of the elite. The corners of her mouth twitched in involuntary distaste whenever she saw the guests smile with their collagen-injected lips and hide behind the facade of high society. The worst was watching Vanya follow Ved everywhere he went, like a puppet led by strings. Hera seemed to be enjoying the show. Raina noticed as she gave Vanya her empty wine glass and whispered something in her ear before sashaying away. Raina couldn't tell if the singer was relieved or disgruntled; the wide smile she had put on since lunchtime was stuck on her face.

Slowly, everyone finished the tour and headed back to Hera's garden, the same one from where Raina had entered earlier with Don. She had learnt while covering the tour that it was the side entry to Hera's mansion. By now, it was lit up with fairy lights, as the sun had started to descend, and bunches of tastefully done-up flowers adorned tables that had been set up for guests. Barbecues and bars had been set up too on movable wooden wagons. The mood of the evening was changing and the music had changed with it. The light notes of a trumpet floated dreamily as people rested on lawn chairs and tapped their feet to the melody of jazz. Raina sat on one of the chairs, exhausted, typing out a short article about the event. Ronit continued filming the event for a few more hours until it was dinner time.

'It's almost eight. I will start homewards soon,' Ronit announced, packing up his gear. 'I've sent some footage and photos to the team; the rest I'll do when I'm home.

The team's already posting pictures and videos. They were going to cross a million views on a few of them as of an hour ago. #GoldenHera is trending on Twitter already.'

'That's the best we ever got,' Raina said. She could imagine Vin's greedy grin with advertisers competing for ads on *Glitterbug*. When he saw money, Vin was like a dog who smelled a bone.

Raina sighed and looked around. She could see some of the guests leaving. Hera was seeing some guests off while her most loyal group remained seated near a steel hearth. Raina frowned. To her, they looked like a pack of wolves waiting for the Alpha to come and initiate the meeting. Here's how we will hunt the powerless people; here's what you all will do to crush their sense of self! It is the command of your leader; live and die by your orders!

Raina observed some of the wolves in their luxurious Italian suits, ties now carelessly loosened. They looked quite inebriated. Would they blurt out something they weren't supposed to? Could she get a definite testimony this time, even if it was from a drunk Hera worshipper?

'Finish up later. Let's pack up,' Ronit said, now zipping his bags.

'What, now?' She tore her gaze away and frowned at Ronit.

'Yes! I intend to take you out for a dinner better suited to us North Indian food lovers. All this fancy food is boring. So are our surroundings. Let's go to Bar Stock Exchange and say cheers to an evening spent without controversies ...'

'Umm ...'

'We're done here,' Ronit said, looking into her eyes with an intensity she'd never seen before. 'You're not planning something, are you?'

'No! Ronit, it's just ... dinner, the two of us ...' she clasped her hands together. 'I'm trying my best, you know that ...'

'C'mon, it's just dinner. An inconsequential date with me. You know how I feel about you.'

His hand was sliding closer to hers on the red silk tablecloth. Something made her curl her fingers; call it a reflex, or an instinct. Even as her cheeks flushed and her body wanted to close the gap between them, she laughed nervously and continued to type, studiously avoiding his gaze.

'Ronit, I want to stay behind for a bit. The atmosphere is more relaxed now; who knows what stories may emerge? I promise, no controversies, and I'll get a taxi in an hour, don't worry about me.'

'You won't get a taxi from here.'

'I saw kaali-peelis parked outside the main gate, probably for the staff. Don will help me book one, or I'll have Hera drop me off in her helicopter,' Raina said with a laugh. 'She'll do that now because I have nothing against her.'

'So, you're done investigating?' Ronit sighed and grinned. 'It's just as Vin predicted. Once you see everything with your own eyes, you'll be satisfied.'

Raina smiled, knowing that the truth was far from it; *the truth was uglier than expected.*

Ronit tried again. 'Raina, I don't want to leave you alone here,' he said, biting his lip as if to control himself. 'I just ...' his hands reached for her curled fingers, 'want to take you out, talk, drive, listen to music ... just spend time with you. Just take a longer step and walk towards me.'

He looked into her eyes. Raina's heart trembled like the strings of the violin she'd seen being played earlier—high, melodic, otherworldly. She wanted to give up everything in that moment and go with him. Her feelings for him were deeper than she had ever felt for any other guy. If she could only try a little more, let her feelings play out—

A man in a navy Italian suit almost fell over as he stood up and went inside the hall towards the washroom. Her train of thought broke. She couldn't help but watch him walk away from the corner of the garden.

'Raina, are you listening at all?'

'I am, Ronit,' she looked back at him. 'I promise you, very soon. I just ... need a little more time to accept things as they are. What about this weekend? Even if I'm not ready in these few days, I will take a chance and go out with you, just the two of us and things that make us happy ...' She wanted him, wanted an 'us', a happily ever after. But she first wanted to finish what she had started with Hera. As she made a promise to Ronit, she decided this was it.

One more attempt. If this fails today, I'll give up. Antara and her cronies can go to hell. I'll find another way into crime reporting. Another way to make Ronit proud of me.

'Not today?' Ronit's smile faded a grade.

'Just today ... Please?' She did what she'd never thought she would do; she uncurled her fingers and took his hand between hers. The fluttering feelings of a teenage romance tickled her stomach. She'd never felt anything like this before, with anyone else ...

'If you say so ... I can't wait for this weekend,' Ronit said with a smile. He pulled her close and kissed her. Raina had a strong urge to leave with him in the car, go somewhere far off listening to a synth playlist and make love, but it would have to wait.

'Don't stay much longer. Try to catch Hera and make up with her,' Ronit said.

'I will,' she said with a nod. He looked hesitant, but she assured him she would leave soon, so he left with one last look at her. She saw him leave, the equipment hanging on his broad shoulders, and sighed. It took her a few minutes to compose herself.

'Okay, let's focus. This is my last shot,' she murmured

as she stood up and walked swiftly towards the washroom.

It was a huge bathroom situated discreetly behind an alcove. As Raina passed, she saw Sarah instructing caterers and cleaning staff. Ved was talking to a young man who was wide-eyed and flashing a bright smile.

Another wannabe, thought Raina, as she stood at the washroom's door.

(Or another victim ... said her inner voice.)

Raina quickly scanned her surroundings. Don was nowhere to be seen, but Hera was talking to an American, standing by the fireplace. In the small alcove, where Vanya had adjusted her breasts, Raina pushed the heavy door and made her way inside the washroom. It was large enough to qualify as a small apartment, complete with a basin with gleaming faucets, shower area and a fitted jacuzzi in one corner. There was even a walk-in closet. There were two toilets, of which one was occupied. A second later, the man in the navy Italian suit flushed and came out. He looked pale and dizzy. His bloodshot eyes were unfocused under the bright lights, and he blinked as he washed his hands. Only then did he notice Raina standing in a corner. His eyes ran over her body, taking in her hip-to-waist ratio and lingering on her breasts.

'Hello there. Who might you be, if I may ask?' he slurred.

'Just a guest ... I've seen you before. Are you someone famous?' she said, flashing a playful smile. He returned a smutty grin.

'Oh, you bet I am!'

'More famous than Hera?' she raised her brow. He snorted, rolling his eyes.

'Who do you think makes sure she stays famous in a good light?'

'I don't know; she seems to do a pretty good job herself.'

'No one can achieve her god-like status alone, little girl! You have a lot to learn. I could teach you, if you want.' His grin broadened, and his bloodshot eyes stared at her chest brazenly. He stepped closer, wiping his hands on a soft towel.

'And what is it that you can teach me?' Raina asked. She giggled in spite of the disgust crawling under her skin.

'Big things!'

'Really? The only big thing I see here is this land,' she scoffed. She was baiting him, and he was too drunk on his power to realize it. Just as she had imagined. He was still staring drunkenly at her cleavage.

'I'm the one who got this big land for her. I get her big things all the time.' He came closer. She could smell the alcohol mixed with an expensive, musky perfume. The fragrance agitated her, and blurred images flashed in her mind.

Clive Christian ...

'How many lives did you destroy to get this big thing for her?'

'Too many questions. I'm not enjoying this.' His grin faded and he frowned at her. 'Are you from the media?'

'Well, not from the kind of media that can hurt you. If you give me inside stuff, I'll keep it anonymous. If you don't, I'll find out anyway,' she said, reaching out to lightly touch the gleaming buttons of his waistcoat. 'Custom gold-plated buttons, huh? Where do you get this kind of money from, I wonder ...'

'Back off. You can't do shit. Blackmail someone who's scared of this nonsense, Miss,' He snapped and brushed her hand away. He turned to march off, furious.

'If Hera were to find out about the way you spoke of her, she wouldn't be happy, would she?'

He stopped abruptly and looked back. A vein in his forehead throbbed.

'You do anything like that, and I'll have your tits cut off, bitch.' He strode outside.

Raina watched the door slam behind him. She took a deep breath. That had not been easy, but it was a lead to something. Investigating the guy would get her evidence, but would it be substantial enough? Ronit's smiling face swam in front of her eyes. As always, the question of priorities hung above her; was it chasing corrupt stars or making a happy life with a man as intelligent and good-looking as Ronit? She decided to sleep on it.

TEETER-TOTTER

When Raina left the washroom, the fireside couch was empty. The sitting room was spotlessly clean, and the extra seating arrangement had been removed. The hall looked bigger than it had at noon. Two regular-sized Mumbai apartments could fit in the sitting area alone, Raina thought. She walked outside and took out her phone to book an Uber; she'd had enough of these people, and it was time to go. The app didn't open. She tried Ola and a couple of other apps, but nothing loaded.

'Shit.' Her eyes fell on the network bars, and she realized there was no signal. She connected to the guest Wi-Fi and tried again. This time the app loaded but showed no cabs in the area. She tried one app after the other—no cars, no bikes, no kaali-peelis or autos. She looked around for Don or Sarah. They were nowhere to be seen. Raina could only spot Hera, standing outside and laughing softly with a few men around here, one of whom was the man who had just threatened her. He was clearly having trouble maintaining his balance.

'My goodness, aren't *you* drunk, Savos?' Hera placed her left hand over her smooth face as she watched him stumble around and chortle drunkenly.

'I—dunno—if ... um ... I'm drunk ... Hera ... What's 'appenin' ...?'

Raina grimaced at the man. How much more did he have to drink after the washroom visit? She saw Hera discreetly gesture to Ved. He supported him at once, hauling his arms over his shoulder, and gently ushered him to a chair.

'I'll get the chauffeur to drop him,' said Ved and disappeared into the hall that led to the main door. This was her chance to get a ride, Raina thought, but then hesitated. Would she be able to bear a two-hour-long drive back to Mumbai with a drunken man beside her? The knot in her stomach tightened, and she regretted letting Ronit go.

'Hera, once again, congratulations on launching this beautiful project. I'm glad I could catch up with you today! You know I'm there for anything you need,' said a man and others soon chimed in. They thanked her, promised to see her again and bowed as they bid her good night. Raina noticed that no one shook her hand or dared to hug her. No one even met her eyes like colleagues. Hera stood tall, right hand poised gracefully over the left, and nodded slightly at each man with the hint of a smile. For a moment, Raina had to admit, her aura was majestic. Her bearing was proud, and her body was a gift from Aphrodite herself.

Hera had covered her bare shoulders with a delicate and expensive-looking pashmina; nights in the greener region north of Mumbai could be cool and foggy. From their surroundings came the rhythmic sound of crickets. Raina was acutely aware of how late it was and that her hands were cold. The inky sky above her looked liquid with floating swirls of grey clouds. The moon was but a crescent, a glimmer of a distant object, blurring in and out of focus as the clouds drifted around it.

Perfect, Raina gritted her teeth, *rain clouds*. She sighed, thinking about how much time she had to make it to the main gate of Golden Hera Farmhouses and find a cab before the rains hit. Surely there would be at least one cab about!

'I thought you'd have left by now.'

Raina turned as Hera's musical voice reached her. The superstar was walking towards her; only it seemed as if she was sashaying down the catwalk with an enigmatic smile.

'My colleague had an early day tomorrow, so he left. Would you mind …' Raina gulped, her cheeks turning scarlet in embarrassment, '… if I asked for some help with the cab? There are none around. I tried the guest Wi-Fi—'

'You embarrass me, Raina. Of course I'd like to help,' Hera said, lifting an inexplicable trepidation from Raina's heart. 'However, there is no one around. Everyone is done for the day, I am afraid. I would ask Ved, but he's had too much alcohol to be trusted with a car, as have I. Even Sarah and Don are needed around here to take care of things.'

Raina's heart filled with a weird anxiety again, the kind that a rabbit must feel when out at night in a jungle.

'Do you have a vehicle I could borrow? I'll return it in a day—'

'If you can pilot a helicopter, it is all yours!' Hera smiled. 'Golf carts won't get you to Mumbai, nor will the horses. Unless you could ride them, that is.'

Raina shook her head which felt like a hydrogen balloon tied to her neck. Why didn't she leave with Ronit? Here she was, begging for a favour from the very woman she despised the most.

If only I had made the right choice back then …

'Raina,' said Hera, making her jittery again. She didn't know what it was, but she felt her confidence melting away in Hera's presence. 'I know we've had our differences. And you are not the only one. I seem to bring out the disagreeable side of many people, though I don't really mind. Everyone is different, and that's what makes the world interesting. Why don't you let me make it up to you?'

'I don't understand,' Raina said and blinked.

'Stay the night, I insist.'

Raina blinked again.

'It's going to rain anytime now, and there is no alternate way out. The chauffeurs on duty are with one guest or another. My personal chauffeur is off with Savos. You saw how drunk the man was. I wouldn't ask Don to drive so late for so long after the day's exhaustion.'

Raina's throat went dry. Stay under the same roof as

Hera for a night? The humidity around her skin solidified into ice.

'Ah, come on, you don't want to be standing here all night, do you?' asked Hera, her enigmatic smile spreading and her eyes glimmering as if she were enjoying their conversation immensely—or maybe she loved the expression of a frightened, trapped little animal.

'I don't think I'd want to inconvenience you anymore—'

'Nonsense! *Glitterbug* will hate me even more if I leave you out here for the wolves—or the leopard that's rumoured to walk these hills at night. It's part of the charm of this place, the wild animals.'

Raina felt like a child up on the teeter-totter, hanging helplessly in the air, at the mercy of a naughty friend sitting on the other end, who refused to let her come down. She was in Hera's territory. She had to smile and nod, do what she asked, and return to the battleground the next day.

Don may have worked tirelessly the whole day, but looking at his straight back and sprightly step, it would've been hard to guess. It did not seem to have affected his energy level at all. He walked as briskly as he had at the race course stands and Raina found it hard to keep up. His eyes were sharp, and his old but handsome face showed no trace of exhaustion. He led her through the sitting room, past the fireplace, and up the stairs towards the bedrooms. Raina was pretty sure no outsider had seen as much of

Hera's farmhouse as she had—by now she had enough stuff to fill up the society pages of the national dailies.

She climbed up the polished, marble stairs. An ornate wrought iron railing, branching out and flowering in black curls, lined the arched stairway. As she reached the topmost stair, to her left, she got a glimpse of another sitting area—the biggest sitting area in the mansion, that was closed to guests—with a huge double door front entrance. She immediately remembered the photoshoots of Hera she had seen in *Vogue*. She also knew from the same shoot that chandeliers—ten feet in diameter, made of diamond-cut glass—hung like inverted wedding cakes and radiated heavenly light over the textured, white walls.

As she crossed the last stair, Don cleared his throat, bringing her out of her *Vogue* photoshoot, and gestured to turn right. They entered a carpeted corridor, decorated with mirrors on both sides. The corridor was warmly lit with ceiling lights and brass lamps. There were four large rooms on the floor, one in each corner, separated by intersecting corridors in the middle. Before she could explore further or see what was there on the other end of the intersecting corridors, Don stopped and led her into the very first room on their right.

'The one next to you is madam's bedroom. She will come up in a while,' Don said and turned to look at her. 'She doesn't like to be disturbed. I hope you understand.'

'Erm ... yeah ... ' she replied, not sure what Don meant.

His sharp eyes glinted with warning behind his glasses.

'Miss, do not come out of your room during the night, come what may and do not make a noise. Keep your windows shut.' He told her gravely. 'I will come to get you for breakfast at around eight. If you need anything before that, please call 333 from the landline on your bedside table. Is that acceptable?'

'Yes,' Raina managed to reply. His piercing look sent shivers down her neck. Did he suspect her of anything? Did he think she would go looking for something in the dark corridors? Thunder rumbled, and rain began to patter against windows at the end of the corridor. The sky flashed in white light like a hungry lion.

Evidence ... what about it?

'Okay then!' The intense look changed into a warmer one, his tone more professional. 'Here's your room. Have a good night.' He opened the door for her and bowed slightly. The lights switched on automatically, as if in a fancy hotel, and Raina could see a huge room waiting for her. She entered after muttering a hurried thanks and goodnight to the butler. An air of uncertainty filled her lungs as she closed the door and locked it from the inside.

It was the biggest room she'd seen in her life. A king-sized bed made of sandalwood lay flanked by matching bedside tables, oriental lamps sitting on them. There was a set of white, deep-cushioned sofas around a mahogany coffee table decorated with indoor plants. There was a large TV mounted on the wall, the shelf below it packed with books. The only thing out of place were two photo-frames lying on the bottom-most shelf, below the books. Raina picked them up for a closer look; a young Hera of about thirty smiled at her with a newborn in her arms and her late husband by her side. He was a tall, thin, fresh-faced man. She couldn't imagine him being an alcoholic or a drug addict from his clear white eyes. What went wrong within a few years for this young couple was beyond her comprehension, though she had theories. The more wealth one gains, the more unbridled the desires become. Hera, however, she observed, seemed to have escaped the lashes of time and didn't seem to have changed much with age or compounding wealth. The second frame was a simple DIY cardboard one with a picture of a teenage Hera with her father.

Now, that was the face of a different person altogether. No semblance of the carefree smile and innocent, gleaming eyes remained on Hera's face anymore. Raina sighed and put the frames back.

She went to the lavish bathroom and ran herself a bath. As she dipped herself into the fitted stone bath full of hot water, only one thought crossed her mind. Should she pursue her search for Hera's secrets or sacrifice it to make a life with Ronit? If she found out more about the man called Savos, she would probably find a big story, but it wouldn't be easy. It could even mean the end of her career as a journalist. On the other hand, she could take the easier path and accept her present job. She could choose to be happy and in love—take it easy. He was in love with her, but he wouldn't stay that way forever unless she reciprocated. She had to make the right choice ...

Choice ... what a strange word, she thought. It felt like a curse.

She rested her head on the edge of the bathtub and let the fragrance of the bubble-bath wash over her.

It was a sweet fragrance of flowers ... she took a deep whiff of it and ran to her mother, trying to jump up to her lap, giggling. Her mother placed a soft, warm palm on her cheeks and caressed her. She was saying something Raina couldn't understand, not at the time. But there was a sense of foreboding looming around them. The sunlight behind her mother's frame blurred everything. She could suddenly taste blood on her lips.

The ferrous smell of thick, red blood engulfed her as she slipped and fell on the floor. Her mother was not sitting on the chair anymore, and Raina couldn't jump into her lap anymore. She could sense a man's figure standing behind her, grumbling, and he suddenly threw a glass on the floor, where the blood was. It smashed into smithereens. A waft of alcohol tingled her nose and settled at the back of her tongue in a bitter taste.

She had to get up and wash her hands. She had to clean the floor, and the walls, and the table from where more blood dripped. What a mess ... She bent and looked at the growing red pool. Her mother was standing over her and smiling.

'It's okay, it's not yours,' she said, and Raina looked at her face—a face streaked with blood that was flowing over a shiny black eye and a deep cut over her swelling lip. Raina screamed and shut her eyes. She seemed to be drowning in blood. It reached her waist, then her chest, then her chin and was now up to her nose.

She gasped and sat upright, flailing her arms. She'd fallen asleep in the bath. The water had turned cold, and the bubbles were gone. She clutched at her chest and took in big gulps of air. It was a nightmare, one that she hadn't had in a while. They'd started when she was sixteen; she had found her mother dead, wrists slit, one day when she returned from school. No suicide note was left behind.

Feeling dizzy, Raina stepped out of the bath. A big, white clock with a brass frame told her it was ten past midnight. She dressed herself in soft white pyjamas that had been kept neatly on the bathroom rack. In the total silence of the room, she sat on the edge of the bed, bouncing up as she did, and stared at the wall in front of her. Whether it was the thought of her never going to get rich enough to own a farmhouse or the discomfort of the total silence, she got up and drew the curtains back.

'Whoa!' she gasped at the beautiful view the glittery grey curtains revealed.

Behind them was a thick sliding glass door beyond which extended a white, marble balcony with a railing as high as her waist. Potted plants and creepers decorated the corners while a cast iron table and chairs stood in the middle. Raina unlocked the windows and slid them open. The humid night breeze, a few degrees lower than the city air, blew across her face, carrying the fragrance of wet grass and night flowers she couldn't see. Hera's vast estate sprawled, disappearing into the horizon, an alienscape under the crescent moon, glinting in the silver light and whispering in a language humans didn't know.

It was breathtaking; it was chilling. A haunting mystery. The hair at the nape of her neck rose, and she gripped the black iron railing. The wind grew thick with whispers as she listened.

A sound of laughter, shrill like a girl's and dark like a conspirator's, came from her left, the direction of Hera's room. Raina turned, moving closer to the sound, straining her ear. The laughter came again, followed by some hushed words. Now there was a second voice, crying. Raina pressed against the railing and leaned towards the room from which the sound seemed to originate. Soft music played inside. She could only hear a few words.

'Do it again ... shirt off,' she heard Hera say, but her voice wasn't the elegant and controlled drawl from before, rather it was harsh and shrill.

Raina froze. Something was happening, something newsworthy. It might be the evidence she was looking for! She reached for her phone in the pocket of her pyjamas. The distance between the two balcony railings, of her room and Hera's, was less than a leg-split. A sudden rush of air flowed, as if trying to stop her, but Raina had made up her mind. She saw no warning in the wind. Her mind was focused on one goal; all other thoughts faded in the dark. She stepped on the decorative twirls in between the railing and hoisted herself up, holding onto the edge of the wall. She didn't dare look below her. It was the first floor, but the distance to the ground was higher than your usual buildings. With a deep breath, she took a wide step and planted her foot gingerly on the railing of Hera's balcony. Her hands cold and sweaty, she let go of the wall and grasped the edge of the wall next door that formed the boundary of Hera's balcony. It took all her strength, mental and physical, to cross the distance, but ultimately she landed on Hera's side like a cat.

Her heart beat wildly; adrenaline rushed through her blood. Hera had pushed the curtains to the sides. Faint moonlight seeped into her room through the middle. Raina moved closer, taking care to stay hidden behind the bunched-up curtain. As she glanced inside, the scene she witnessed shocked her.

Hera, wearing a slinky satin baby doll dress, sat on a couch watching a man dancing around a pole. The man was dressed only in thongs and heels, with a full face of make-up. He was gyrating on the pole to music that Raina recognized to be from Tchaikovsky's *Swan Lake*. She would have dismissed it as an act of consensual sexual fantasy and role play if she hadn't recognized the man's face—it was the wannabe actor chatting up Ved earlier that evening. So, this is what they had to do to get the job. Raina felt a wisp of anger rise amidst the adrenaline. She angled her phone the best she could and started to record everything she saw. The dancing man had a red collar around his neck that was attached to a leash that Hera pulled at periodically, taking an almost orgasmic pleasure in the act.

'Dance like you mean it, Swan, because your life does depend on how well you entertain me while I wait,' she said and laughed, pulling the leash so hard that he fell mid-twirl. Raina gulped. The man looked scared and ashamed but determined to get through this as he stood up almost immediately and poised himself against the pole. Raina wondered why the man complied. Did he think he would get out of this? More importantly, what was Hera waiting for? The muscles in Raina's arm had started to complain after twenty minutes. She had recorded enough evidence she decided, and retreated with the phone safely inside her pocket. She stepped on the railing with one foot, held the wall for support, and kept the other foot on the next railing. This time, she faced the window of the corridor wall separating the two rooms. In the clear sight of the intersection of the corridors, she saw yet another fantasy playing out. It was Ved and Sarah, wrapped in each other's arms, gasping and moaning as they made out on a table in the corridor. Just this morning, he had been flirting with all those women! Raina screwed up her face, befuddled, and continued. Maybe the whole family was crazy, she thought.

'Ahh!' she gasped as she lost her footing and slipped. Luckily she managed to cling to the railing and now dangled from it. 'Oh God …' she whimpered, looking around and then below. If she could manage to lower herself by holding the bottom bars of the railing, she could land on the grassy lawns below without too much physical damage. If only she had trained her arms well in a gym, she could have hauled herself up, but currently, her arms were trembling, and her hands were slipping. Raina contemplated trying to swing a leg back up, but the thought of falling down at an odd angle put rest to that. It was quite a distance, but she had jumped boundaries before in pursuit of stories.

'Damn it,' she cursed through gritted teeth and let go of the railing.

Raina groaned as she pushed herself up. Her ankle was slightly strained. She frowned at her muddy hands and feet and stained pyjama bottoms. She wondered if she could sneak back into her room undetected, but knowing the steely-eyed Don, that was not an option. What excuse would she make if he caught her? That she fell over the railing? Did someone see or hear her fall? Before she could process, a light went on in the room she had landed in front of. She quickly hid behind some bushes. From where she was crouched, through the glass panes of a window left ajar, she saw Don enter and signal someone to follow. Once more, her jaw dropped. Savos followed groggily, knocking a floor lamp down, shattering it instantly, and slumped on a couch near the window, muttering something barely audible. Raina thought she saw his lips form a 'sorry', but all she heard was gibberish. Without much thought, she started recording the scene.

'Perhaps you are sorry, yes … but the fact that you erred shows you are, well, drunk,' said Don. Raina frowned. What did he mean? Surely, he didn't say that to Savos for knocking off the lamp. Also, Savos was supposed to have been sent home with a driver. What was he doing here?

Savos seemed to struggle for words but gave up with an exasperated sigh. He tried to get up but fell into the couch.

'What've ... you ... given me?' Savos struggled to say each word.

'Something to dull the pain.'

Silence fell, sharp like ice. Raina saw Savos go pale and shake his head. The next second, Don raised his right arm, and a loud voice stabbed Raina's ears. She screwed her eyes shut for a moment. When she opened them, trembling, she saw that Savos had a hole in his head. Behind him, the smooth white wall was splattered with red. Everything slowed down around her. The blood froze in her veins. She shivered uncontrollably where she crouched, holding her clattering mouth shut with one hand and recording with the other.

'Ah, there he is, all ready for me,' she heard Ved's booming voice as he entered the room and stood inches away from Savos, looking into the dead man's petrified face. He sounded nothing like the polished and classy young man from before; in fact, he sounded quite mad. 'Sarah, clean him up for me. I'll prepare him for the exhibition. This one's going to be so special it's giving me a boner!'

'Yes, love, let's finish this soon!' Sarah had entered the room and was standing beside Don. Raina could almost hear the lascivious grin in her voice. Sarah walked towards the dead man, held his face between a thumb and finger, and turned it towards herself.

'Hmm ... His lips are hideous. Sew them tightly for me?' she said and let go of the face with a jerk. Don, who had suddenly gone missing from the scene, reappeared with a wheelchair and, with Sara's help, picked up the dead man and dropped him into the chair.

'Plug the poor bastard, will you? The carpet will get stained otherwise,' Don frowned. Sara produced a black garbage bag from her apron pocket and put it around the lifeless face. Next, she pulled out a wire and wrapped it around his neck, securing the head.

Raina shook like a leaf against the wall outside. She could watch it all, record it all. There was no way she could return to her room after witnessing what she had. She'd have to find a way around and run away without getting noticed—

'Raina, is that you? What are you doing outside?'

An electric current ran up her spine. Raina looked up. Hera was leaning against the railing, looking down at her with amusement.

'I'm sure you couldn't have heard the gunshot in your soundproof room. Did you, perhaps, leave your room despite being told not to? Hey Don!' Hera called out.

Don turned into the direction of Hera's voice and spotted a terrified Raina. He grimaced and walked to the window, sliding it fully open.

'I warned you,' Don said as he pushed his glasses back over the long bridge of his nose, glaring at Raina.

Run! shouted a voice in Raina's head, and she took off without a second thought. She had a head start. They'd have to get out of the front door at the other end or break the iron grill of the window to catch her.

She had put her phone in her side pocket and ran like there was no tomorrow, not caring that she was barefoot running on the ground with small rocks, not looking back lest her courage faltered. She would run all the way to the safety of her little flat if she had to. She would push anything and anyone in her way. She'd scale the boundary walls and clamber over the gates if need be. She would hide somewhere they would never find her. All she knew was she had to flee.

The grass provided some friction in the wet mud, but it was difficult to run any faster. Rocks, dried twigs and possibly night-crawlers armed with stings cut the skin of her feet.

They'll bite, they'll poison, they'll make you fall—

She shook her head to dispel the horrible thoughts in her head, drawing deep breaths as she ran to keep herself charged up for the marathon ahead. From a distance, she heard the barking of several dogs; they were loud, merciless and hair-raising. She turned in a panic and saw a pack of four hounds and three Rottweilers chasing after her. The whispering woods had gone silent except for the loud barks that echoed all around.

In her state of fright, Raina forgot to draw deep breaths

and the strength to run the marathon ebbed away. No one could outrun those beasts anyway. They drew nearer, till she could feel their hot breath on her heels and hear their teeth snapping close to her legs. Fear took over as Raina started whimpering, shaking and stumbling on her feet. Finally, she slipped, like the voice in her head had foretold. The dogs immediately surrounded her, leaping over her and barking into her face. At last, a blood-curdling scream escaped her throat. They gnawed at her arms and legs, forming short gnashes as they tore into her skin. She curled into a ball and tried to shield her face and torso. Hot tears flowed into the manicured ground, as Raina spotted the main gate, just a little ahead. The dogs scratched her and barked at her with bloodshot eyes burning in scarlet fire.

Raina thought they would rip her apart with their teeth, but they did not bite.

After what seemed like hours, but was actually ten minutes, two golf carts smoothly came to a stop in front of her. Don and Sarah got out of them.

'Sit,' Don commanded, and the dogs immediately sat, growling and staring at their catch. 'Look at you, all mud and blood. That was a new silk night suit.'

'What a waste,' Sarah said and shook her head in pretend sadness. Then she pointed a rifle at her head. 'Don, you know I'll do as you say.'

'And I will do as the lady of the house says. We will take her back.'

'No, no, no, no!' Raina cried and shook her head, refusing to uncurl her body. Don bent towards her, hands on his knees, staring at her like she was a mushy caterpillar he could crush between his fingers.

'Would you rather I command my pets to tear you apart? If I say the word, they will shred you to pieces. A rather painful death, trust me.'

The dogs growled menacingly, attentive to their master's tone.

Raina whimpered as she shook her head miserably.

'Thought so. Sarah, tie her up.'

FIRE AND EYES

The wire that Sarah had used to tie Raina's wrists cut into her flesh. It seemed to be some sort of metal wire. Even slightly shifting her position made her wince. That didn't stop Sarah from roughly pulling her out of the golf cart and shoving her into the main hall of the mansion where she'd had lunch just that noon. The strength in Sarah's arms was that of a well-trained combatant and not someone who was only engaged in housework. Raina shuffled along, not daring to even squeak. The decorations, people and scenes from the afternoon seemed like a distant dream from another life. How she wished she'd left when she could have! What in the world had made her stay back?

Foolishness, not ambition …

'Make her sit away from the carpet,' Don said. He frowned at Raina's clothes caked with mud, grass and blood. Her footprints had left dirty marks on the polished marble. Sarah grunted in reply. They entered the sitting area around the fireplace where Hera was waiting, comfortably reclining on a plush couch. She had covered up her translucent baby-doll dress with a silk kimono.

'Here comes the little spy. Thanks, Don! Well done, Sarah,' Hera said, looking into a book in her lap. 'She can sit beside the fire while she curses her fate.'

Don bowed slightly, and Sarah smirked, dragging Raina away from the carpeted area and towards the fireplace.

'Squat on the floor like a good bitch,' Sarah spat menacingly and pushed her down.

Raina's arms were burning with cuts, and the fire made it worse. She couldn't stop a shaking cry and tried to move away from the three feet tall and as wide a fire.

'Sorry for the rough treatment, Raina, but you asked for it. Don't move from the spot, or I'll have to increase your punishment,' Hera said as she closed the fat book she was reading. She leaned back, folded her long legs, and watched Raina squirm.

'Look at you. What a sorry mess! Why didn't you simply stay inside the bloody room? I never wanted to have you tied up like this, no. I only wanted you to write a favourable article for me. You knew too much. Winning you over would have been a victory in the eyes of my fans.'

'I don't believe it,' Raina said through the tears of pain. 'You would have paid them to shame me for being an attention-seeker, a liar, who now got back to her senses. You would then have come publicly to forgive me and wish me well. Fans would exalt you for being the better person.'

Hera sighed, disappointed, though her eyes gleamed as if she were looking at an exquisite piece of art in a museum.

'You are quite something; you know me so well,' she said and leaned closer. She perched her porcelain face on her palm. 'Were you watching me? Before you saw Savos croak? How did you even get down from the balcony?'

Raina stayed silent, her teeth biting the inside of her cheek to keep her from crying. A roaring thundercloud announced rain, and it started pouring, like an infantry charging with bayonets.

Only if the rain had started a few minutes back, probably Hera wouldn't have spotted her, Raina thought, cursing her luck.

'Why are you silent? Don't you have anything to say now?' Hera's grin faded to a grimace. Sarah slapped Raina, almost knocking her to the floor.

'No blood splatters, please,' said Don, sternly watching Sarah.

'Sorry, she makes me want to beat her. I don't like her face,' Sarah said. She grabbed Raina's hair and pulled her up, making her squeal in pain. 'Hera asked you something. So *speak*.'

The three of them stared at Raina and watched her whimper. Fresh tears ran down her cheeks, making streaks across her dirt-covered skin. Sarah rolled her eyes and looked at Hera for instructions.

'Why …' Raina managed to croak. 'Why did you kill Savos?'

'Ah … She speaks.' Hera's face lit up with a mad, wide grin. 'He had it coming. I was too patient with him, but today, he crossed a line. He tried to act cool in front of you, at my expense, just to get you in bed. Of course, the fool didn't realize at first that you were tricking him!' Hera laughed. 'All but he knew you by face. I have no need for such idiots.'

'How ... how do you know that?' Raina couldn't help but stare at her in shock.

'I have my ways. I can find out whatever I want to about whoever I want, anytime I fancy. Except you,' Hera said. She stood up and walked towards a centre table. A wooden tray lay on it, holding wine bottles and crystal goblets. She held one goblet up, and Don immediately poured some wine into it. 'You never say what's on your mind. No matter how much I tracked you, I never figured out what you really want.' She swirled the wine gently and sipped, filling her palate with the flavour.

'Tracked me? Were you spying on me?' Raina couldn't believe what she was hearing.

'Home, office, everywhere you went,' Hera shrugged, sipping her wine and pacing around the table.

'But how can you ... Why would you need to? What does that accomplish? I—'

'Hush, hush ...' Hera said as she sipped again and watched Raina, as if searching for something in her watery eyes. 'You are interesting, that's why.' She walked closer to Raina. Hera's presence was more painful than the hot wire cutting into her wrists. Raina wanted to move away, but her back was against the fire. 'You see, no one else has ever dared to cross me. You didn't stop at the article, even when shit hit the fan. You didn't back off.'

Raina gulped. Hera's porcelain face was inflamed with fury. Was the world blind not to notice? The rain outside intensified, accompanied by loud eruptions of thunder.

'You, a worthless little girl, kept on raising questions and investigating without a sliver of fear. I hated it, but I also liked it. It's good to come across someone like you once in a while. It reminds me of my youth.'

'Your youth was nothing like mine. You were brought up in a house made of gold!' Raina spat back despite Sarah's grip over her hair. 'You don't know pain like I do.'

'Don't I?' Hera's eyes crinkled in humour. 'Don't we all in some ways? Some more than others?'

'Not you, no,' Raina shook her head defiantly. 'You were born with a silver spoon up your ass—' Sarah yanked Raina's hair tightly.

'How dare she! Let me shoot her in the stomach!'

'It's okay, Sarah, let her speak,' Hera said. The smile on her face widened.

'You had it easy, you inherited wealth and movie contracts, and you inherited your father's legacy,' Raina gritted her teeth. 'You don't get to say you suffered, bitch!'

Hera kept a hand on Sarah's shoulder; she was about to reach for something in her apron, probably a wire to suffocate Raina.

'How it pains me to hear this from you, but it is hardly your fault. No one knows what I have carefully hidden for all these decades. Right, Don?'

'Right, madam,' he said, his head slightly bowed.

Hera moved a pouffe closer to Raina and sat inches away from her. Raina couldn't say if it was pain or madness on her face. Her crazy smile was still there, though.

'I will tell you secrets, Raina, that no one knows about me, except the people in this house. My father didn't leave me wealth, precious metals or a "gold house". All he gave me was a broken family, debts and a forced contract that barely saved us from living on the streets,' Hera said as she gestured to Don to pour more wine. 'I was seventeen when the contract was forced on me. My dear daddy traded me for money with legendary producer and director Balram Dixit, who was looking for a fresh face for his movie. You'd think it was a win-win, but no. In the agreement, between the lines, there was a clause I didn't know about. That clause concerned my body.'

Raina watched her take longer sips of wine, as if trying to swallow the bitter fact. It left a scowl on her face.

'He had these lustful eyes, a lecherous way of looking at me, and dad knew it. Dixit got an opportunity to get a pretty face for his movie and for his lunch breaks during the shoot. When I told my father that it was unfair to his minor daughter that a fifty-year-old rape her every day of the contract period—because he had to fuck me in my vanity van to keep it a secret from his wife and kids—my father kept his hand on my shoulder and asked me to bear with it. "It's just a matter of three years, Antara. You know we have no choice,"' Hera snorted, after mimicking him, and continued.

'The first day, my first time, was horrible. I cried. I tried to fight him off. He beat me. Spared my face, thankfully. The next day was worse as he was prepared and even more aggressive. It kept going on and on, him raping me and my father asking me to bear it. My mother asked me to be strong because women always have to struggle, especially when we have a *legacy* to save … but why did I have to suffer like other women?' she frowned and sipped her Bordeaux.

Raina was dumbstruck. Balram Dixit was an icon of Indian cinema and had been adorned with accolades few achieve in a lifetime.

'It was ridiculous, me giving in like common women do. I was so naive,' Hera shook her head, frowning at her teen self. 'It took me time, but I figured out how the world works. You know it, don't you?' She turned to Raina. The look on her face was crazier when she didn't smile. 'The thing that works like magic is nothing but an illusion, a trick. It is fear ... Deep down, people want to believe in something supreme, something high above their common reach. And anything superior like that causes fear. They need to fear you to worship you. To respect you. That's the only way to make it in this ruthless world. Only gods make it through the wars, Raina. Commoners all die. Only if they see you as all-powerful do they respect you,' Hera went on as Raina stared at her slack-jawed.

'The world shakes in fear in front of a non-existent god and thinks nothing of life that's present in the now. So, I devised a plan,' Hera said. 'Why not kill the repulsive old man and continue with the rest of the contract with his son? The son, Rajiv or RJ as you would know, was handsome and in his thirties. Much easier to manipulate too. He'd fear losing me, a very important part of his father's project, with so much money at stake. I found him much more acceptable for the vanity-van routine, too.'

'But Balram Dixit died of a cardiac arrest!' Raina almost whispered.

'Oh, no, little bug! Not really. I made it happen. I made his erotic fantasies come true to the point that he became dependent on me. He even wanted to renew the contract! I was ecstatic to see him moan like a pig at my mercy. At the end of every day, I'd give the pig a small dose of poison that eventually led to a cardiac arrest in a matter of weeks. The pathetic old man went out with a hard-on in a whore's bed somewhere in Juhu. His wife was shocked, but she hid it all from the press,' she said with a giggle, sounding almost like a teenager.

'But you didn't marry RJ ... he ...,' Raina's eyes widened. RJ had died in an accident in Los Angeles.

'Of course not. I didn't have to do much with him. He was under my thumb right after his father's funeral. While shooting for the second movie, I dominated him completely. He was easier than his daddy, you know, fell right into my trap. He adored me, worshipped me, but I was bored of him and refused to renew the contract. When I left to model in LA, he came to see me every fucking month! His dick needed me. Can you imagine it? It was getting annoying. I had someone else in LA, someone more handsome and more useful. RJ was just garbage,' Hera scoffed in disgust.

'What did you …' Raina was almost scared to finish that sentence.

'What did I do? What do you do with garbage? I challenged him to drive to the Hollywood Sign in reverse gear after one very satisfying night. Of course, he was high and thought he would prove his love by performing a silly stunt. We were miles away from the point. My friend in LA made sure he fell in a ditch on his way,' Hera said with a laugh.

'Your friend? Do you … you mean your manager, Desmond, who got you modelling and music video contracts?' Raina gasped. 'How could you?'

'How could I? How could *they*?' The fire in Hera's eyes flared momentarily. She sipped more wine to put it out. 'RJ wanted to curb me, tame me. He wanted me to admit I was in love with him. I wasn't! I was tired of these demands, these attempts to control me. Nothing comes out of being good. You know that better than anyone else in this room. Desmond could do anything for me. And he did. He was a good manager, and he knew I would rise with one solid movie! Only if he hadn't gotten arrested—'

'He was arrested because he stabbed and killed a person,' Raina snarled. 'Was that you, too?'

'Desmond stabbed a casting director who refused to let me star in a movie I wanted. He wouldn't let me bribe or fuck him, because he believed it was his job to get it right. Something had to be done. Desmond only did his job. I got the part and the fame that came with it. Cheers to that!' Hera raised her glass.

'You are twisted', Raina said. Sarah kicked Raina in the side this time, making her bend over and groan.

Don sighed and repeated, 'No blood on the carpet.'

It's okay, Sarah. I am twisted, and so is everyone I know in showbiz,' Hera said with a chuckle.

'Not at all, madam. She's uncouth,' Don interjected.

'Raina, do you know why I married a dull man like Abhiram Malik?' Hera asked, sipping more wine.

'You had the money ... So why else?'

'Oh, probably you didn't research enough. Well, Desmond was out of the frame, RJ was dead and I needed more power to expand my kingdom. The power I wanted came with more money than I had. Abhiram was desperately in love with my image on the Hollywood screen. We met at a party in LA and hooked up. I'd say he fancied that one night so much he wanted it to be every day of his life,' Hera said, laughing at her own joke. 'I thought it wouldn't hurt to marry a billionaire. But ... let's just say he didn't like my growing ambitions. Abhiram wanted me to take care of our baby and stay home. He didn't even agree to me being a part of his management! His reason was that people saw me with "different eyes", and he didn't like it.'

'If I may add,' Don said, 'he was an insecure man who was scared that madam would overtake him in his own business.'

'The gap between us was irreparable by the time Ved started walking. He found solace in other women. It was unacceptable.'

'So you killed him too?' Raina asked, pale in horror by now. 'Half of this land, your office building, your properties, and so much more, all belonged to him.'

'So what? I gave him many good years, Raina, and I gave him a son. Do you know what he gave me in return?' She leaned so close that Raina could hear her furious breathing. 'He cheated on me. Finding solace was one thing, but falling in love with another woman? And just so you know, his business wasn't flourishing. Go smell his financials with that detective nose of yours and you'll see a mountain of losses that *I* recovered from later. Competition was burying that Neanderthal. He wouldn't heed my advice to enter showbiz! All he wanted to do was stick with his failing tradition.'

Hera chugged the remaining wine in her goblet as she watched the fire crackle behind Raina with a scowl.

'What did he do instead? He argued with me, made bad decisions, incurred more losses than he had in a decade and got a whore as his new woman. Ved was two when his stepsister was born and brought into this household,' Hera said and pointed at Sarah. Raina's insides churned with repulsion as she recalled the scene from the corridor.

'Like Zeus, that vengeful god,' she spat. 'He tried to keep me chained to this household. He made deals with people to convince them not to work with me, thinking it would tame me. I had to teach them all a lesson, of course, but dealing with that dickhead came first. If it wasn't for Don here, I don't know how much longer I would've had to suffer.'

'You made him overdose ...?' Raina sputtered.

'No, I just laced his drugs with some poison, the same invisible stuff that causes cardiac arrests. He was not a user, so I had someone introduce him to drugs,' Don stated as if reading from a textbook.

Raina watched him in cold horror. Don, however, stood straight and nonchalant as ever.

'He left me no choice. Anyway, all's well that ends well,' Hera said and smiled, satisfied and glorious. 'I am Hera, and I am to be worshipped, nothing less.' She stood up and went back on the couch, crossing her legs in a graceful move.

'Why are you telling me all of this?' Raina's voice was reduced to a shrill whisper.

'Why indeed?' Hera said as she tapped her wine glass. 'Take a guess.'

Raina watched her, lost.

The soft squeaking of wheels interrupted Hera. As the rain continued to patter against the windowpanes and lightning crackled, Raina watched Ved push a stretcher mounted on a movable patient bed towards where they stood. A body lay on it, covered from head to toe with a spotless white sheet.

That's how they'd brought mom out of the morgue ...

A crazed grin sat on Ved's face. He no longer looked handsome; the soft glimmer in his eyes had transformed into a pit of frenzy. He looked wild and untameable—a beast raised by Hera answerable only to her.

'Mother, I cleaned him up, just as you like it. The canvas is ready!'

'That was fast. Well done!' Hera smiled and handed him a glass. Sarah let go of Raina's hair, pulled on a pair of neat white gloves she carried in her apron, and poured some wine for him, holding his gaze.

'Don,' Hera said. 'Pass the tray.'

Don approached with another wooden tray, full of strange little bottles filled with brilliant dyes, a box containing needles of different sizes and many rolls of leather.

'What have we here!' Hera picked up the leathery rolls in her hands and compared them, muttering something to herself. Ved watched her in excitement. Sarah stood on guard above Raina, pushing Raina's chest back every now and then against the hot chimney wall. A stoic Don watched everyone.

As Hera finalized what she had to do, she clicked her tongue and gestured to Ved to switch on the chandelier above them—a thousand bright yellow bulbs fitted in a concentric crystal structure—and pulled the white sheet. On the bed lay a dead and yellowing Savos, drained of all blood, his lips stitched as if painted for Dia de los Muertos celebration. Raina shrieked, inviting a rough shove from Sarah. She was pushed closer to the fire that instantly seared the upper layer of her arms and singed some of her hair; she could smell herself burning alive. The pain was agonising.

'What the fuck are you doing to him?' she screamed. Despite the fear she felt, her anger and frustration felt like they would explode. Burns on her skin aggravated her.

'Stop the drama. I need to focus,' Hera frowned as she unfurled a roll in her hand. Sarah pulled Raina's hair again and gripped her face tightly between her fingers. The cold metal of a gun touched Raina's neck. She stopped struggling.

'One more word and you'll have more holes than you were born with,' she said menacingly.

Sarah had switched to a revolver. She held the gun in the same hand that she was pulling Raina's hair with. The pocket of Sarah's apron was bulging at the bottom. Raina could glimpse the tip of a brass bullet when she strained to look out the corner of her eye. If only she could break free ...

Break free ... she wouldn't have had to if she had only made the right choice and left this infernal place when she had the chance. If only she hadn't been greedy for news, like she was greedy for—

'Here we go!' Ved cheered, twirling the wine glass in much excitement. A few drops hit the carpet, and Don winced.

'I'll be a moment, madam,' he said and vanished. Hera was too busy to notice. Under the bright light of the chandelier, Raina could see Savos lay still. He wasn't leaking blood anywhere anymore. It was as if he was unconscious with a bad case of jaundice. Hera flattened the roll with her palm and cut out rectangles.

'Do you know what it is?' she asked Raina. 'This is the skin of the woman who let every man do her to get little rewards. She was Savos's whore. His wife knew nothing about her. Savos introduced the girl to me and asked for a favour. He wanted me to let her do a dance number in my movie, because she was so beautiful.'

'One of the most beautiful women we'll ever see, to be exact,' Ved said and snorted.

'Yeah, and he was talking to *me*. So, Raina, even if he hadn't done anything to upset me today, his time was already up. The girl is alive, don't worry, but she'll never get a chance in showbiz again.'

The downpour intensified. Raina stayed silent and let the sky do the screaming for her. She didn't want to imagine what part of the woman's body this crazy woman had stripped clean of skin.

'Now, I'm giving Savos the most exquisite thing in his life. I'm making sure he's one with the love of his life forever,' Hera said with a grin. Uncontrollable laughter escaped her lips. Ved and Sarah followed suit.

Three laughing psychopaths ... if she ever got out, she would learn to paint and make a portrait with this title, Raina thought. Silly things crossed her mind as she saw Hera sew the woman's skin over Savos' chest. It is weird how the mind tries to save itself when witnessing horrors.

What painting would describe you? a small voice spoke in her head. *A fitting end for you, Raina, would be painted in the fire of hell and in the reflection of madness. Three Laughing Psychopaths and a Girl Who Didn't Know Better.*

Raina closed her eyes and bit her lip as if doing that would calm her irregular heartbeat and sweating. Yet, despite the ominous echoes of laughter, something made her inch closer to the fire. She'd either die trying out a ridiculous idea or die just waiting for the worst. Sarah's grip over her hair had slackened momentarily, and she did not notice Raina shift closer to the fire.

You won't get rid of your foolishness, Raina, even if you live ...

Hera had taken a larger needle and a thread and was patching the flap of human skin over Savos's deflated chest. Raina moved her wrists closer to the fire, muffling a scream. Don had still not returned, so she had a chance. Sarah was watching the process in awe, and Ved was sipping more wine as Hera sewed on the patches in different positions and shapes until Savos' chest resembled something like abstract art.

'Now for the face,' she said gleefully.

Raina had seen enough morbid movies to know that the set of lashes Hera had picked from the tray was human. A bit of skin was still on them. It made her intestines knot in disgust and, with the added trauma of the fire burning her wrists, made her want to pass out. Anything to stop seeing this or feeling the fear she was witnessing.

Witness … I am a witness …

Yes, she was a witness, and she had evidence. She could get more evidence if only she could escape. She had to get a grip. Biting her lips once again, she tried to pry her wrists free. The pain tore through her nerves, and she sweated like a pig.

Once Hera was done with her patchwork, she picked up a brush and dipped it in one of the wide-mouthed bottles. A whiff of rusting iron emanated, a smell Raina recognized from the day she saw her mother stare at her blankly, sitting in a pool of her own blood. It made her sick to the stomach. Hera hummed *Danse Macabre* as she painted over the patches of skin with blood. Ved moved his finger like a symphony conductor. Sarah watched him with a smile. Don came back and started cleaning the wine spots on the carpet. Raina worked at freeing her wrists at intervals, slowly but steadily. The wire was cutting into her flesh, almost to her bone, and her vision was blurry with tears and pain, but she finally seemed to be getting it to loosen. Metal expanded in heat; that was basic science. No one but her seemed to remember.

'Now, the indigo and the golden … ' Hera muttered, oblivious. 'I want to sew the eyes open, but I don't want them cloudy. Don, you have contact lenses? Black?'

'Yes, madam, right away.' He stood up and walked into the kitchen beside the hall where lunch had been laid.

'Sarah,' Hera continued as she painted, 'thanks to you, the skin is without cuts and stress. Good work.'

'Thanks,' Sarah's cheeks flushed scarlet, and she took an ecstatic, shaking breath. 'I succeeded in making you happy; that's all I want!' Tears shone at the corner of her eyes, and her face was that of a devotee who had seen god smile. It creeped out Raina even more than the morbid patchwork of skin and artwork of blood. An involuntary grimace appeared on her face. Sarah noticed and shoved Raina hard, letting her fall hazardously close to the fire. Raina fell over on her face. Her right cheekbone and eyebrow took the brunt. Her hands pulled apart, and she screamed in agony. Almost immediately, she calmed herself, noticing that the wire had loosened significantly. Her wrists were covered with blood and burnt skin. With some zig-zagging motion, Raina could finally squeeze one hand out from the wiry loop.

'What's taking Don so long? I want to do the eyes now—'

An explosive gunshot made Hera and Ved drop on the floor, covering their ears with their hands. Don came running towards the couch. His eyebrows furrowed into a deep, dark line when he saw Sarah on the floor, covered in blood, the pouffe overturned beside her.

In one sleek move, Raina had grabbed the revolver, pointed it at Sarah and pulled its trigger. As Sarah fell, gasping for breath, she grabbed a handful of bullets from Sara's apron, and ran away towards the staircase she had taken earlier.

Some bullets rolled out from Sarah's apron pocket over the marbled floor printing their trail in blood.

'No!' Ved screamed when he turned to see Sarah bleeding on the floor. His voice boomed in the huge sitting room, cutting the downpour and rumbling clouds. Sarah rolled onto her side, taking in a rattling breath, and pressed the side of her neck with a hand.

'My neck ...' she barely whispered.

Hera gestured for Don to take her threads and needles as he came running towards her. He sprang into action.

'Ved,' Hera turned to her son. Her face was a deep shade of maroon. 'Get that bitch to me. Alive. You can do whatever you want with her after I am done punishing her.'

'I intend to, Mother,' he said, his jaws clenched and face a dark shadow. With a last look at Sarah, he stormed to the stairway flanking the left of the fireside. He reached for the hidden drawer under the stairs and pulled it out. It revealed a secret armoury. The finest guns, small and large, shone alongside boxes of bullets. Ved took two handguns, loaded them and tucked them into his belt. He took a shotgun and hoisted it over his right shoulder. To punctuate the foreboding scene, he tucked daggers into his boots.

Just a floor above, Raina stood on the familiar corridor, shaking. She could peek downstairs and see through the grill. The Grim Reaper was coming for her. Only this one had bullets in place of a scythe.

Up in the air on the far side of a see-saw ...

A girl who couldn't run when her feet were on the ground.

LOVERS

Raina knew she had to act fast. She moved towards Hera's room at the end of the corridor. A blipping green light indicated there was a CCTV camera installed. She broke it with a brass vase ... and looked to see if there were more, but she didn't spot any. This floor had four rooms facing each other, divided by intersecting corridors. Another corridor led away from the room into an open space. With time running out, Raina decided to dash into that open space, farthest from the corner from where Ved was coming up. In the faint moonlight falling slant inside, she could see a big couch, a coffee table and lines of bookshelves. The walls were mainly glass from floor to ceiling. Unfortunately, there was no balcony for her to jump out beyond the glass wall. The rain subsided by a fraction and the inky sky had ghost-ships of clouds sailing nowhere. Raina could hide in dark corners, but not for long. She came across a work desk as she moved around the bookshelves, trying to find the darkest corner with some space to hide in, and instinctively pulled the drawers. A metallic rattle suggested a key. Raina pocketed it. If there was a key, it had to lead to a door. She walked around the work desk, keeping Sarah's gun pointed at the entry to the room. All she had to do was hide, avoid hitting anything, and hold her breath till she had a head shot.

'Raina!' Ved's voice boomed as he walked in the intersecting corridors outside. 'I know you're here. You broke the CCTV? That is so smart of you!' he said, ominously sweet, and clapped. Raina moved towards the dark spot opposite the windows, across the work desk, where the moonlight didn't reach. As if answering her wishes, cloud-ships began to sail slowly in front of the moon. The cold, silvery light faded. An obsidian shadow plunged the room into darkness. 'But was it the only one, Raina? Was it?' Ved's voice rang aloud.

Hair stood like quills over her skin. Her eyes darted from one dark wall to the other, to the corners, over the shelves. Were there more cameras or was he bluffing? Certainly, she was in a dark corner, but would that save her? She swallowed, as if to consume her fear, but it stuck in her throat like a stone. Back to the wall, revolver pointing forward, she went still. Ved's loud claps, hoots and jeers faded into a distant echoing voice that filled her head.

No one escapes forever ... your mother did not, I couldn't, and you won't either ... you will see, you will face the consequence. Consider it a cursed gift, for that is all I have to give you ...

A shadow, darker than the inky room, loomed over her

eyes. She froze as the shadow took the shape of a man—a tall, bulky man who she had feared the most all her life—and became more defined as the cloud-ships sailed away. The shadow surely would reveal a chiselled, stone-hard face with a scar over the right eye. The shadow would turn into her father as she scrambled to her feet, trying to drag herself away from the pool of blood and the blank stare of her mother. As she tried to shout for help ... as her father walked deliberately towards her with a knife in his hand and a grimace under hollow eyes ...

You don't run forever ... You only run out of life. Like your mother. So, accept your fate. Stop trying—

'—to escape!'

She shuddered and gripped the gun with both her hands. Ved had come very close to her. He had searched around the couch and the coffee table and was now approaching the shelves, steps away from the work desk. He hadn't bothered to switch on the lights; it was more fun hunting prey in the dark. Or perhaps he feared being shot by his hidden prey. Raina was confident of the former reasoning.

Blood continued to run down her elbows and drip quietly onto her pyjamas. Yet, she didn't dare let her gun down for even a second. As Ved paced around the bookshelves and Raina shrank back further, something hard struck her back. A doorknob. Raina remembered the key. Would it fit inside this? If she tried the door with the key, it would definitely alert Ved, and even if she slipped inside, her Grim Reaper would shoot a hundred holes into the door till she bled out.

But Hera wants you alive ... No easy death for you!

Right, Ved wouldn't kill her yet, but he could shoot her. It would be painful, but Don would fix her for Hera, whatever that may mean. Her head ached and her shoulders hunched in a sudden spell of vertigo. The gun drooped lower.

Just shoot the bastard, just shoot the mad bastard!

'I'm running out of patience, bitch. The longer you make me wait, the harder it's going to be for you. I'm going to make you beg for death. I'll make you cry me a river!' His voice got deeper and darker. Done with jeering and taunting, he cocked two long-barrelled guns in each hand and shot blindly.

One shot and two. Bullets dug holes in the walls.

Raina shook, somehow biting her lips to keep from yelling. She knew his position, she could shoot him, but she was petrified. She noticed the wetness that had spread in her pyjamas. There was no way she could aim straight and shoot the beast dead in her state. Ved fired again. Her knees gave away when the shot hit the work desk, and she growled in madness.

'Come out, you piece of shit! Wriggle out of your hole! I'll shoot you in the neck, let Mother sew you up and then open your guts myself before you die,' he heaved, eyes bloodshot. 'I'll dissect you alive.'

Raina whimpered. A bloody hand rose to her mouth, and the other limp at her side over the revolver. It was no use. Her body wouldn't listen to her. He was working his way around the desk, shifting closer to her inch by inch. Shaking and devoid of all options, she took out the key from her pocket and inserted it quietly into the keyhole above her head. The key turned, and the door opened. What next?

Go inside, hide. Lock yourself. At least you'll have time to shoot yourself in the head and be done with it! You don't run forever ...

The beast, the Grim Reaper, was now steps away. She wanted to crawl inside the door and lock herself up, but her body wouldn't move. A spell of blackness covered her eyes, and she jerked herself awake as adrenaline spiked. She couldn't go unconscious now, even as her burns made her feel like it.

You only run out of life.

Ved was now very close. She could almost feel his movements. Her skin was rigid and thorny like cactus. The sweat on her body seemed to have frozen. She opened the door behind her. It creaked slightly, ever so softly. Ved turned slowly towards the door. The corner was dark, and he had to stare to check if the door was open or closed. A grin spread on his face, ear to ear. His eyes glazed over in craze. He closed in towards the door, enjoying each moment before he caught his prey. The thought of sinking his claws into fresh, juicy skin gave him the pleasure no orgasm ever could. Not even Sarah could give that to him.

'I spy with my eye ... Where's the dirty little spy?' he sniggered. 'Say you give up, and I won't shoot you right now, I promise ...'

It happened in a split second. The moment he closed

in on the door, he tumbled over Raina crouched on the floor. With a jerk, he fell on the door, which swung open. It was a miracle for Raina—not that he fell inside what seemed like a wardrobe, but that she could struggle out of the grasp of darkness. A miracle that she could shut the demon in her head and finally pull the trigger. Her hunter screamed in pain and Raina took the chance to lock him inside. A barrage of bullets came flying out of the wooden door with deafening explosions. She escaped by the skin of her teeth and ran towards the couch, away from the flying bullets, and loaded up her gun with shaking hands slippery in her blood. The chamber had two bullets left. She stuffed in seven more from her pyjama pockets.

'Fuck this shit, fuck this shit,' she chanted in a trembling voice, too shrill and breathless to be her own. The rain started to bombard the windowpanes once again. Thunder rolled. Lightning struck the sky in red and green, looking like the veins of an angry giant. Was there any way she could jump out of one of the windows? She walked along the walls, ignoring Ved's cries—he was howling like a mad dog and trying to break the door—and walked towards the windows, assessing the possible risk. She was too high up. If she survived the jump, she was sure to break her bones and be caught and ripped to pieces by the hounds. Either way, there was no escape.

A low growl distracted her from her thoughts. The sound was just like the one she'd heard only a few hours ago out in the grounds, when she was trying to escape. Air escaped her lungs, and she realized it was no hallucination. Two eyes shone in the dark, locked in her direction, moving slowly towards her. Soft footsteps followed the hound.

Don.

The butler didn't utter a single word. She could smell death again.

Run, when your feet are on the ground, run!

Without thinking, without letting her demons whisper in her ear, she shot at the hound and dropped beside the couch as a bullet sped through inches away. The hound was now howling. Soft footsteps moved to where she was, so she crawled the length of the couch to the armrest on the other end. She couldn't see Don in the dark, while he had the advantage. Any time now, the hound would jump onto her, and she'd be caught. She waited for her doom, gun pointed in front. The least she could do was empty the bullets into her attacker ... but nothing happened. The hound made no sound. Did she hit it?

Clouds sailed past the crescent moon, and Don's glasses reflected some of the silvery light. He was looking for her at the other end of the couch. Within a split second, she took aim and fired. Raina's bullet got his arm. He grunted and aimed his shots at the armrest, closing in the gap. Raina rolled behind a single-seater couch beside her and aimed again. This time, Don ducked and leapt on the one-seater.

'Arghh!' Raina screamed in agony as the couch toppled

and she reflexively put her hands up to protect her head. Don stood over the toppled sofa and took aim at her. She froze for a second. Before he could pull the trigger, she sat up with her arms over her head, still holding the revolver, and pushed him as hard as her wrists would allow. The pain galvanized her insides, and she gritted her teeth. Don rotated his arms but couldn't balance over the plush couch. He fell on the glass centre table, crashing the back of his head into it.

Raina tried to stand up, but she fell as another spell of darkness covered her eyes. She was losing too much blood.

'No … no, no, no, no, no, no …' She shook her head and blinked. 'Stay awake … talk … walk …'

Don was twitching and groaning. She pushed herself up, hands over her thighs for support, and forced herself to walk. She pocketed the guns Don had. Then, she searched him and found a pocketknife, which she shoved into her bra, an untimely recollection of her grandmother doing the same with currency crossing her mind. Her toothless smile was all she could remember from when she was six years old, and her granny was ninety. What had she said then, when Raina had come back crying?

She shook her head, blinking heavily and crying in pain now, and rummaged through the drawers of the bookshelves hoping for some first aid. Luckily, she found tissues, bottles of alcohol and cotton rags on the lower-half of the shelves. She used them to clean her wounds and cut the rags into bandages with Don's pocketknife. She cried all the while, taking deep breaths to calm herself, but finally managed to bandage both her wrists. She cleaned her face and disinfected the cuts on her cheekbone and eyebrow bone.

The face-off with Don had given her more scratches and cuts, but they were nothing in comparison to the trauma she had gone through in the last few hours. On the same lower shelf, there was some leftover water in a crystal bottle beside the expensive, imported alcohol she had used to disinfect. She drank it in massive gulps and took a deep breath. Loud noises came from inside the closet where she had locked Ved. It was only a matter of time before the beast came running outside with more reason for vengeance. Despite all the gunshots and other sounds, Hera had not made an appearance. What could she be doing, Raina wondered. Definitely not wilting in a corner! Could she have any more accomplices? The thought made Raina shudder again. She had found a box of aspirins between the alcohol bottles. It was time she swallowed some and got going. If only she could sneak out without facing Hera, she'd be safe. She had enough bullets to shoot the hounds. The golf carts—she remembered from lunchtime—were parked in front of the swimming pool, just beside the main exit of the mansion. The only problem—she was quite a distance away.

'Shit …' she turned towards the centre table as broken glass tinkled.

Don had regained consciousness and was rolling to his side. She checked the gun she had taken from him. It was loaded. With a deep, shuddering breath, she got back up. She felt more sure of herself, stronger with the bandages on and the beast still trapped behind a wooden cage. Blood of the dead hound glinted on the floor as the sky cleared once more. The rain was falling on the ground instead of the glass now, as the wind dropped. Don's eyes flickered open. Thick, maroon streams flowed down his eyebrows and neck, soaking his crisp white collar. His eyes were still sharp like a predator's.

'You think,' he said in a hoarse voice, 'I'm the only one who gets the bets right all the time? You don't know Madam Hera.' The corners of his lips twitched into something between a grin and a grimace. 'You will lose this game. Your time is up.'

'We'll see about that,' she said and pointed the gun at his face, and hooked her finger at the trigger.

'Isn't it so easy to pull the trigger?' Don said with a grin, as if amused. 'So easy to keep running, turning a blind eye …'

She gulped. Her hand shook. She started as a loud doorbell rang twice.

'Don't you want to see who's at the door?' he asked and chuckled. Raina shook her head, 'You are only trying to get in my head.'

She frowned, beads of sweat forming on her forehead. What did Don mean?'

'Ronit! What brings you here?' Hera's voice came bright and cheery, from a walkie-talkie Don had stuffed in his trouser pocket.

Blood ran cold in her veins once again. Don's chuckle turned into laughter. He had to keep a bloodied hand over his mouth to stop himself.

LIES

'Hi Hera!' Ronit smiled as he stood at the huge oak main door.

'Ronit! What brings you here? And so late? Oh my god, you look tired. Come in first. Let me get you a drink,' Hera said as she smiled brilliantly.

'Oh, please don't trouble yourself,' Raina heard him say in a nervous tone.

On the other corner of the house, Raina felt numb with foreboding. He was inside the house and standing near Hera. What should she do? What she couldn't do was escape alone.

First, she had to deal with Don. She wanted to shoot the butler once and for all, but instead, she tied the man up with a telephone cable, tearing it off the wall along with the plaster and paint. Hera would not hesitate to kill Ronit if he suspected anything or tried to locate the source of the gunshot upstairs. There had to be another way, something she could do to warn him so that they could escape while they still had time.

Once she had tied up Don, she walked towards the other end of the corridor, back to the staircase she had come from, with Don's gun clasped between her hands. Ved seemed to have grown tired of trying to break the door or—better—had choked on his tongue. She kept walking to the end of the corridor, beyond the staircase, and reached the end. There was a room on her right. She rotated the doorknob and the door slid open effortlessly.

The room was dimly lit, with lights coming through the sheer curtains. Raina didn't dare switch any lights on. She walked in silence towards a French window in the room which, according to her understanding of the lay of the house, must overlook the main hall. Raina hid in the corner of the window and moved the curtain an inch. She could see Hera sitting on a plush white couch a good distance from her, in a grand hall.

'I uh ... I don't know how to put it ...' Ronit had taken a seat beside Hera, who was nodding, listening intently. 'It's two, and Raina hasn't answered her phone, messaged me or logged online even once. I called the security of her building, and they told me she hadn't gone home either. I got worried and started asking around. No one's heard from her. Would you know anything of her whereabouts?' he asked with a nervous smile.

'Well, of course! You think I'd let her go alone so late at night? I made her stay back. She's upstairs in one of my guestrooms.'

'Thank God,' he said and exhaled in relief. 'I'm sorry I didn't know who to call in here, and it was my mistake to leave without her. I've just been so worried. Sorry, I bothered you.'

'She's such an angel, honestly. I'm glad she stayed back. It gave us a chance to really understand each other.'

'That's wonderful ... she didn't mean you any harm. She was just doing her job.'

'I understand, and I think let the past be in the past. Let me call her. Raina! Look who's here!'

'That is not necessary. I'm sure she's fine,' he said, rubbing his nose, the colour rising in his cheeks.

Raina could see Ronit shift in his seat, looking nervous and worried at the same time. Then, her eyes fell on something else. The glow from the nightlights in the hall was enough to make the gun tucked at the back of Hera's silky nightrobe belt shine. Raina's lungs collapsed for a second. The only way out was perilous.

'It's no problem. Her room is on the first floor.'

'It's all right. I'm sorry for the intrusion, but I'd rather she slept.'

'I highly doubt she's asleep. Looks like she's made rather good friends with Ved and Don up there! They are watching some movie, action and whatnot!' Hera said with a girlish laugh. Ronit rubbed the back of his head, laughed sheepishly and looked around. The news seemed to have upset him. What would he think about her? They were not dating officially, but spending a night with Ved and Don, two men she barely knew, would sound like ...

Fuck it, Raina! That's a problem for later. For now, run with him!

You can't run forever.

Shoot Hera and run!

The brutal voice in her head was damn right. She had to shoot the bitch and rescue her man. Adrenaline surged through her body, and she readied herself for the hunt and rescue. Before Hera could reach for her gun and hurt Ronit, she would shoot her dead. She toughened herself up with grim resolve, and she went down the stairs.

'Raina! Will you come down or should we come upstairs?' Hera said loudly and chuckled. 'How sweet you two are,' she said, shaking her head and sighing, pretending to be moved by young love. Meanwhile, Raina was moving carefully towards them. She could hear the wood crackling in the fireplace. In the state of absolute awareness, Raina could hear the wind blowing outside and rustling the trees. The rain had stopped but temporarily; the clouds were still rumbling. The arched entry to the hall was just a few paces ahead.

'Kill you ... kill you ... bitch ...' she jumped at hearing a sudden raspy voice. She'd forgotten Sarah, who lay on a couch, gritting her teeth and growling at her.

'Dream on,' Raina whispered, flashing her eyes at her as she continued inching towards the hall, bracing herself for the impact of the gunshot on her wrists; the impact from the gunshots before was still painful.

She crouched behind the curtains of the arched entry, hidden behind pillars and vases as tall as four feet with arrangements of reeds and paper flowers. After the vase, there was no other shield for her, and the hall was huge, like a ballroom of some palace. She had to shoot Hera without harming Ronit and run.

'Ronit, why don't *you* give her a shout? Just by the stairs of the fireplace,' Hera said with an enchanting smile, pointing towards the fireplace.

'Okay, but maybe she has fallen asleep? I don't know if I should disturb her,' Ronit said as he walked towards the fireplace.

Good, now I'll shoot her—

Just when Ronit stepped between the two of them, Raina saw Hera slip the gun out of her robe and point it at Ronit's back.

'No!' she screamed and jumped out of the shadows. 'Ronit, step aside!'

'Raina!' Ronit jerked back in shock. His arms went up reflexively. 'What are you doing? Is that ... a gun?'

'Oh my god! What's going on?' Hera gasped and put a hand over her chest. 'Raina ... what is this?' Her other arm slipped the gun behind her back, a finger ready on the trigger.

'Hera, stay behind me, please,' Ronit said. His heart was racing and cold sweat rolled down his forehead soaking his pinched eyebrows.

'You don't understand, Ronit,' Raina screamed. 'Hera and every member of this house is a murderer! I saw them kill Savos ... do things to him! I saw her torture a boy ... he's still upstairs! Look at me, Ronit, look at my wrists, my face, my clothes! This is all their doing!' Tears fell afresh from her swollen eyes, the eyebrow with a cut almost bulging out. 'There was no action movie. It was Ved and Don shooting to kill me. I have evidence. Please trust me. I was right about her ... Let's get out of here right now. Hera, drop your gun, now.'

'What are you talking about? You make no sense—' Hera sounded confused.

'Now! I mean it, Hera!' she shouted, her face blazing hot. Even though her body was trembling with nerves, her hands were steady and her eyes fierce. For a second, Hera did pale.

'Calm down, Raina. What has happened to you? We can talk. See? I have no gun,' Hera said in that same baffled tone. She raised both her arms above her head, looking scared and vulnerable. Ronit got more agitated. Only Raina could see the glint of madness in her eyes or discern the shadow of a sneer on her face.

And fear ... she is afraid for her life.

'Turn around, you bitch, turn!' shouted Raina, gesturing with her gun at Hera's chest.

'I will step aside, Raina. Please don't shoot! I don't know what you have done upstairs—'

'Oh, for god's sake, there's no one saying action here—' Raina spat out.

'—I'll do as you say; just leave with Ronit.'

'Hera—' Ronit was trying to pacify her.

'She's acting. You'll believe it when I show you everything. Walk back outside, Ronit. Stay behind me!'

'I can't believe you are doing this.'

'I can't either. They tried to kill me! Please, just walk back towards the gate!'

Raina's face creased under the pressure. Her heart drummed a war tune. It took every bit of energy to stay focused on Hera's movements. If she tried to shoot, Raina wouldn't hesitate to pull the trigger first.

'I don't want to shoot, Hera. Stay still and step away. Ronit and I will pass through that gate,' she warned, sidestepping towards Ronit.

'Do what you want,' Hera's voice trembled and tears shone through the evil glint. 'Please just leave me out of this!'

'They should see you now, the Oscar team,' Raina scoffed. She took Ronit's arm with one hand while still pointing the gun at Hera with the other. She walked backwards to the gate with Ronit.

At last, the mighty Hera had been thwarted. She stood like a statue as Raina walked away with Ronit. The distance between the two increased. A few more steps and she could breathe easy, thought Raina. She'd finally escape and expose the four murderers.

Or so she thought.

A huge hand covered her mouth with a thick cotton cloth. The sharp smell of chloroform choked her throat, pierced her lungs and sucked at her consciousness like a leech. Raina tried to claw the hand away. Her eyes rolled, and she looked up. Ronit's beautiful, brown eyes stared back, crinkled in pain. He watched her shocked expression, choked her scream and uttered a single sentence as she faded:

'I'm sorry ...'

No way, no way, no way in hell! I'd rather have died than seen this ... Ronit ...?

She strained against him, rolling and pitching like a boat caught in a whirlpool, trying to stop the poison from spreading through her breath. Hera saw the events unfold with glee. It was like a play with an anti-climax; the hero turns villain, Anakin of Earth, in the house of Zeus who Hera had killed. She now held sway over them all.

The very thought made her chuckle. The chuckle turned into ludicrous laughter that made your hair stand on end in fright. She held the sides of her stomach, watching Raina's eyes glaze over with tears of pain and waves of unconsciousness. The laughter was a distant echo to Raina. She knew who the voice belonged to but the eyes she saw confused her.

With a last horrified look of disbelief and hurt, she slipped like sand on the floor. The gun fell out of her hand. Hera couldn't stop the fit of laughter while Ronit watched Raina's body go limp.

She would always remember May 17. It was a beautiful day, the day she had found out that a handsome senior from her school liked her. She had managed to find part-time work at a cafe. The work was simple; serve the customers coffees and food, and bill them correctly. Her uniform, provided by the owner of the cafe, was cute too—a white T-shirt and a pleated red skirt with buttons on either side. Luckily, her white school sports shoes matched the get-up perfectly. A few thousand a month and a cheerful place, away from her depressed mother and angry father, seven days a week, from nine in the morning to five in the evening. What more could she want?

She was tired of trying to cheer her mother up, tired of complimenting her for the food she cooked, the things she did for them, her beautiful face and smile … tired of her being tired of the abuse her husband showered her with every day.

For a man who had lost his job twice due to anger management issues, whose mental situation got rougher with every jibe, taunt and mocking comment, her father still held tremendous sway over their household. He was angry with everything in the world, right from being born to parents who couldn't provide him much in terms of education or wealth, to the way society was changing, to how his only daughter was growing up so fast and how his wife looked older every day. The surging rage overflowed into his profession, and no one was safe, not his colleagues nor his friends and neighbours.

She wanted to step away from that black despair and be somewhere, anywhere, else. She wanted to get away from that cage, out of the house with only sufficient lights not to knock over the furniture, and breathe freely. She had told her parents that she was going to be sixteen and needed to start being able to provide for her share in the family. She had smiled at her father.

Her smile … Yes, that was the barrier between her

father's volcanic mind and her. Though later, she would find her smile had caused something darker to surge in him in those days she thought her smile was a protective charm.

As if luck had favoured her during that school summer vacation, a boy called Vik, a senior at her school, had joined the cafe as well. On day one, they had both looked at each other with surprise, and she thought of it as a coincidence. It was on the sweet seventeenth of May that Vik had confessed.

'Honestly, I got this job to be with you,' he had said, blushing, stealing glances at her, his hands clutching a rag he was cleaning the coffee machine with. His almond skin was tinted red and his ears were a deep scarlet as he spoke to her. She had felt a sudden wave of warmth wash over her, making her stomach feel fluttery and her head light.

'I didn't want you to be alone in a place like this, where so many boys can see you, ask you out,' he said and cleared his throat. She was amazed at how the slight movements of his throat made her feel funny in the pit of her stomach, how his chest rising up and down inside the crisp white shirt made her mouth go dry.

'Really?' her voice came out in a hoarse whisper. He had a handsome profile. Silky hair fell over his forehead, and his chocolate eyes twinkled dreamily. Unlike the other boys of his age, Vik's skin was smooth and had no marks of teenage skin. He could be a Korean model, a movie star or an idol. His voice had a boyish charm.

In an instant, she had imagined a world with him; a family with two kids—a boy and a girl—and a dog in a comfortable house with a car parked in their garage that opened automatically, set in between greenery and clean air without any negative feelings like anger or depression. She'd be a great wife and take care of their kids; he would be a great husband and kiss her once he'd come back from work before dinner.

'Yeah ... I-I like you,' he'd finally said, looking into her eyes. His soft, warm gaze melted her. She bit her lips, trying not to grin awkwardly.

'Will you go out with me?' he asked earnestly.

'I ... yes!' she glanced at him, red in the face, and replied in a soft whisper even as an opera was going on in her mind, with the violin and piano ...

Piano ... they had a piano in their small apartment. It was an heirloom passed on from her paternal grandfather to her father, who had tried to repair it himself and sell it but did not get a good price. It was too battered. A few keys were missing, and it needed to be tuned. As much as he tinkered with it, it seemed to break down even more. He just wasn't good with the instrument.

'What good was his genius with this piece of useless hulk when he couldn't even leave a dime for me,' he would mutter under his breath every time he tried to fix the piano.

When his wife suggested that he get it fixed professionally to either sell or play it for some money, she was beaten black and blue. He kicked her and broke two of her ribs with the small hammer he had been holding to repair the dented chrome lining on the dark-mahogany piano. But that was not all. The poor woman had to give in to his overtures in bed, even with a broken body.

Raina knew. She had heard the screams that escaped her mother before she muffled them, as the bed in her parents' room creaked violently. She had heard her father's loud curses, and tears of fear had rolled down her cheeks.

So, after saying yes to Vik, as she walked back home, she couldn't help feel a slight uneasiness. Vik wouldn't do that to her, would he? Her father was every bit a handsome man. When he was young, he must have been as charming as Vik, if not more. Did she really know Vik? Would she also have to simply bite her lips and muffle her screams?

No ... I won't ever do that. I'll run away. I'll run right out of his hands ...

Her father had dainty hands but with stone-like knots on his fingers. Vik's smooth hands with soft, straight fingers didn't come close in description. But to Raina, every man seemed to have those stony, knotted hands. They could choke you, thrash you, kill you.

She got off the local train at Andheri and walked about two kilometres till she reached the intersection before her apartment building. After carefully crossing it, her earphones still plugged and playing metal to drown the murky thoughts away, she walked straight till she reached the boundary wall. The building to her left was a posh, rich people's building with a lift and security guards. Her building on the opposite side was old and decrepit. Big flakes of paint had puffed and fallen from the walls sodden with dark green mould, left on the walls by the notorious Mumbai rains. The boundary wall was broken in places and in dire need of repair. The whole building complex wore a ramshackle look. One would know right away that the place was never taken care of. Weeds, shrubs and wild plants flourished between the boundary wall and the potholed road, as well as at the corners of the rusty iron gate that creaked loudly when she pushed it open. Gravel crunched under her shoes as she made her way from the gate onto the narrow path that led to the building. The uneven stairs leading up to the first floor were just cement and bricks, lit by a weak yellow bulb. Patches of dampness formed rings on the walls; like the trunk of a tree, when cut through the centre, you could tell just how many years the monsoons had inflicted damage on the structure.

She made her way to her apartment on the third floor; the only one in the building without a grill or a mesh door. The lock on their door was an old, round chunk of steel that would discourage thieves by its very appearance—how could one find anything worth stealing in a house where folks couldn't afford a new lock, leave alone an iron gate? There was not even a chain lock or a peephole to stave off a robber or a murderer.

The door was unlocked. Her father must've come back early; he didn't like to lock the gate till it was time to sleep. She sighed before pushing the door and stepping inside. Dull rays of the setting sun were falling through a window in the small hall decorated with an old sofa set and cheap crocheted covers. A soft breeze made the washed-out, ragged curtain bulge and fall. The dust particles danced in the golden beams. She was about to take her backpack off and put it on the table when she saw it.

Right where the sunlight pooled, on the little table in the centre, her mother had pressed her ear on the smooth wooden surface. She wasn't blinking. Her eyes were wide open, staring at her in a shocked silence. Her lips were slightly apart as if trying to say her name but frozen in the moment. The dust particles and the light fell over her head and spilled over at the table, over the thick red liquid spilling from her head.

Raina's breathing stopped for a moment. Her voice froze into a lump in her throat; only some wheezing sounds and whistles escaped her. Her eyes slid down and saw an arm hanging limp from the shoulder, slit at the wrist. A knife with bloody handles leaned against a bloodied palm. Its shiny, silver tip was dipped into the blood. The wrist was still pumping out the red liquid.

Raina's legs buckled under her, and she collapsed. The edge of the red pool of blood had reached her shoes. A scream finally escaped her throat. She pushed herself away from the blood. It seemed like a living entity, full of death, moving fast to engulf her. Eat her whole.

She heard heavy footsteps approach and a cold hand with knotted finger joints touched her shoulder. It was her father. His eyes were bloodshot. The red veins in the white of his eyes were remnants of the blazing rage he had no doubt unleashed on her mother. It could lash out at her, too, any minute, any second. Instead, he appeared calm.

He squatted slowly, staring into her eyes with a cold glint but not really looking at her. He seemed to be looking beyond into the next few moments, thinking of different scenarios and what he would do to her.

'Your mom was a mental wreck. She tried to run, and I tried to stop her. She fell and hurt her head. I was preparing to take her to hospital, but she slit her wrists too deep. Much too deep, and now, she's dead. Your mother killed herself.'

'Dad—'

'That's what really happened,' he said. He shook his head mournfully—mournful but also satisfied now that the story in his head had fallen into place—and sunk his fingers into her frail shoulder. She gasped and bit her lips.

'She was suicidal. I have called the police. Tell them everything. Everything about just how it happened ... And let me tell you something, Raina. Some people think they can run forever, but instead, life runs out of them. They try to escape, but it is impossible. A caged bird dies if it tries to carry the cage on its wings. There was no escape for your mother. She was mentally caged. Trapped in her own thoughts and feelings. She tried to run away, and life ran out of her, see? She killed herself trying to run.'

Raina was shivering at the iciness in his sharp voice—deliberately low, stressing on each word. The pool of blood she was sitting in was a mere addition to the terror.

'A woman should know her place, won't you agree, my dear?'

She gulped and moved her neck, trying to nod.

'Good, you must know your place, too. Know it, know your place …'

She didn't go back to the cafe again. Vik never got to meet her after that day. At school, she avoided him twice, and that was enough for him to stop pursuing her. After trying to message and call her a few times, he gave up. There was no dramatic confrontation, no scene like in the movies where the hero tries to win back his lady love. He never stopped her in the corridors, asked a friend to help or dropped letters in her bag.

His last message was: 'I thought you liked me back. You didn't have to embarrass me. Goodbye.'

She wanted to tell him everything—what happened that day and what she was going through—but the reminder of the icy hand on her shoulder was too real even when she was alone in her room. She didn't dare confide in anyone. But it made her feel terrible. Hadn't she decided not to get caught in the trap like her mother? She couldn't stop the tears from rolling down her cheeks.

She had remembered something from her childhood as she cried. Something that had made her aware early on of her position in the world. Raina was five or six, in junior kindergarten. She was on a seesaw with a senior kindergarten kid. The boy, she remembered, planted his feet on the playground and wouldn't let her come back down. When she had kicked her legs up in the air, he had only laughed at her.

'You look like you'll really wet your undies! Paddling

your legs won't help. Haha! You can't push yourself back down.'

'Let me go! Let me down, you smelly turd!'

'You called me *what*?' he roared, his plump, round face screwed up in anger, a reflection of his future male ego. 'You'll pay for this. Stay up there. I won't let you down until you pee. Wet your bloomers, little miss prissy pants. If you want to be lowered, you better beg me.'

'Shut up, fatass!' she screamed at him and wriggled uncomfortably, awkwardly hanging mid-air.

The boy had guffawed, taunted her and ridiculed her, but hadn't moved his feet. She was in a pink frock and ballerina shoes, with a matching headband. He made fun of her attire, her face, her body and her white bloomers that he could see from below as she wriggled like a caterpillar stuck on a twig.

Up in the air at forty-five degrees, Raina could feel her face getting hot and her arms going numb. She was growing tired and freaking out. Her wails and screams did not reach the kindergarten teacher at the end of the playground. Finally, some kids had to go and pull the teacher's jacket to complain about how much noise she was making.

The horrified woman had got her down and consoled her while shouting at the unrepentant boy. He was not allowed to play at the swings for a whole week. The punishment made things worse. He and his little cronies took to bullying her every chance they got. Sometimes they would flip her skirt up, and sometimes they would push her into the mud. Kids stopped hanging out with her, scared of getting the same treatment from the boy and his gang.

When Raina had asked for help from her mother, she had simply smiled and told her she needed to be strong enough to tackle her own problems.

'That's what you get if you provoke men,' her toothless granny sitting on the sofa and knitting a sweater had said.

The entire episode had traumatized Raina more than she admitted, and even years later, she was scared of seesaws ... and men. The feeling of helplessness often came back to her, and she could hear the boy's mocking laugh inside her head. Coupled with the terror of her father and what he could do, she would remain in her room for days. Fixing meals, cleaning the house, readying his clothes for the office, washing utensils immediately after meals and pouring his whiskey every day were her chores now. For hours, he would make her clean the house as he sat watching her. His eyes would scan her body, and she could feel his stark stare.

It had been months since his wife had died and he had had no one to beat up. So, one day, he had given in to his anger and beat his boss. Of course, he got fired. The next time he had beat a man in a bar and run away, fatefully uncaught. The third time, he simply slapped her for not scrubbing the floor properly. The fourth time, he beat her everywhere but her face. If she dared to cry, he would hold her by the neck and pin her on her bed.

A month went by. Her body had become black and blue with marks of abuse. By then, she had become pretty accustomed to it—her father would beat her and she would muffle her cries. It wasn't every day, though. There were good days when he didn't touch her, but these were fewer.

A year went by in this way and another year arrived. The peace was about to end, and her high tolerance was going to become a curse. One day, what she feared almost happened. As she poured his drink, the glass fell from her hand.

He beat her again and pinned her arms over her head with one hand. His fingers were against her throat.

'You are not my daughter … you are not …' His eyes bulged. They were red balls inflamed with rage. She wanted to scream even as she felt like passing out. He was choking her hard, and it took all of her strength to draw in air. 'Your mother was a whore. She had an affair before you were born. Otherwise, why would I feel this way?'

Feel what way? She was confused for a few seconds before the horrifying realisation dawned on her. What he did was worse than death to her. In a frenzy, he undid her shirt and pulled her jeans down to her knees. He stripped her of her underwear, then choked her just enough, while he started to jerk off. She saw him moan and groan over her, his eyes rolling up as if possessed by a demon.

She could feel the violent movement as his frame vibrated like a prong. He almost strangled her to death when he reached his high. Then, he heaved loudly and stared at her bare body. He shook his head in disgust and left her in a terrible state—coughing and crying for the rest of the night.

She knew that the next time would be worse.

However, the next time never came. It never did, because Raina had—

A faint scream messed the memories her unconscious mind was playing.

A distant buzz of voices stirred her awake. She fluttered her eyelids, dazed and confused. Cobwebs were sticking to her arms. She felt the spindly legs of a dozen spiders making their way around her goosebumps. Before a shriek could escape her mouth, she bit her lips, just like she had with her father. A ferrous tang in her mouth made her nauseous, but she had to stay silent like a corpse.

The floor she lay on was cracked, and her back hurt. The dryness in her throat made her want to cough, but she controlled herself. A door opened with a sharp creak somewhere above her and she could hear someone come down the wooden stairs, dragging something heavy.

Thud … thud … thud …

Another door opened a few steps away from her; she could tell as bright yellow lights flooded her eyelids. If it weren't for her long hair interwoven with sticky cobwebs covering her face, she'd be caught. The rain outside seemed to have stopped.

'Ready?' growled the man dragging a living body.

'Yes … she will be next, I assume?'

'Yeah,' he said and suddenly broke into a weird laughter, very hyena-like. 'I'll take my sweet time to work on her,' he said at last.

He pulled a jute sack with one hand as he limped forward.

Sweat covered Raina's skin, every pore crying in fear, and her heartbeat ran like the racehorse she'd seen win that morning. Every cell in her body screamed, begging her to get up and run far away from the cursed estate.

How she wished she had made the right choice when she had had time …

Everything came back to her more clearly. Ved was dragging a person inside a jute bag, and Sarah was waiting for him in the bright room. He had got out of the closet and was back in action. Sarah seemed to have recovered enough to move. The next recollection made her heart wrench in pain.

Ronit …

Her lips quivered, and tears threatened to erupt, but she drew a deep breath and wriggled her arms. Pain shot up from her wrists. She could feel metal wires digging into her already injured arms and legs. She was like a stuffed vegetable wrapped around with a thread before it is thrown into boiling hot oil. Like a deer caught in an anaconda's coiling grip. Her neck was sore, and the side of her pelvis ached. She had no clue where she was or how long she'd been there. It looked like a basement, and she felt like she had been unconscious for hours.

She felt hot and sticky. Slowly, she moved her head. Her brain swam, and she felt nauseous, but she could make out a small glass vent through which some moonlight seeped in.

It was definitely the basement. There was none when she had covered the tour.

A phone rang, chiming *Danse Macabre*. She heard Ved talk in an excited tone. He was jumpy, happy about something. His manner convinced her that he had to be talking to Hera.

'Sarah, she's allowed me to carve her up. Once you clean her, Mom wants to take her pictures, and then she will hand her over to me! ME! I mean, she did manage to bruise me. I will bruise her bad as well,' Ved said, unable to keep the joy out of his voice.

'All in good time, my love. Can you get her here for me? To clean and dress?'

'Right away,' he said. Raina heard them kiss. 'I'm glad you got up. Without you ... I cannot be sane!'

'Hush ...' Sarah's voice was soft, like a coy lover's.

'She will pay for hurting you,' said Ved.

'She must, and you'll make her pay.'

Raina shuddered. What had they planned for her? What kind of godforsaken torture awaited her? Ved's heavy footsteps made the wooden flooring creak in places as he walked over to where she lay. Raina acted like she was still out of commission. He halted inches before her and exhaled in disappointment.

'You'd have enjoyed this more if you were awake. I certainly would've,' he said. She knew he was sneering like Cujo above her. He bent and picked up the end of a rope tied to her ankles. Raina felt a jerk of pain before she was dragged. Every joint in her body seemed inflamed with pain. She bit her lips once again and tried to control her frenetic breathing. Her eyes were still hidden under the sticky tentacles of hair, hiding her creased brows and tears. The wires dug into her flesh, ever more on the left side where she had rolled as he dragged her. She was dumped in the corner of the bright room.

'My, my. I can't believe she slept through all of it,' Sarah said. Her voice had lost its power and sharpness. Sarah had escaped severe damage—the bullet had touched and gone. Even so, the gash it left was deep and swollen. She was heavily bandaged and looked pale.

A sudden splash of ice-cold water made Raina gasp in shock.

'Well, she's awake now!' Ved mocked. 'All bright and fresh after a nap.'

He had turned a knob and water sprang from a hose in his hand. It was so cold that Raina felt her chest spasm and collapse. Then she shuddered aggressively. Ved laughed. Sarah grimaced at her.

'Clean her up nicely,' she hissed.

Ved moved the hose up and down her body, from head to toe, until all the blood and grime had been washed away. Her skin turned whtie with a tint of blue. Her teeth clattered loudly.

'Make her stand up and take her clothes off,' Sarah said.

'I'll help to hold her up and tie her limbs. You take the clothes off. I don't want to see her. No one but you,' Ved said and pulled Sarah close.

Raina watched as he held her with care. He looked into her eyes and then kissed her passionately. A part of her ached inside—a part touched by a cold worse than the freezing water. The madman was loyal to his madwoman. Maybe, it took madness to really love someone, she thought, because love doesn't follow logic.

Ved turned his attention to her. He made Raina sit upright on a long bar stool in a corner and cut her coils open. Immediately, blood flowed into her numb hands and put her in searing pain. She shook, tired and gasping for breath. Her body hurt all over. He made her stand against a round, wooden cut-out fitted with four cuffs, like a tabletop against a wall, and clicked the cuffs closed at her bloodied wrists and ankles.

'Your turn to dress her up in the costume. I'll wait outside.'

What costume? She wondered with a fading sense of consciousness. Her reserve of fear was exhausted or, more likely, frozen. Reality seemed liquid, changing shapes and distorting. The colours were all blurry and blending in front of her eyes.

'You really thought you'd get away? Get evidence?'

Sarah said in a weak but spiteful voice. She took out Raina's phone from the pocket of the pyjamas she was now wearing and waved it in front of her face before putting it back. 'You are so going to die tonight. We'll torture you to death.'

Raina watched her speak those words solemnly.

'Torture me, yeah?' she said, slurring like a drunk, and chuckled groggily. 'Bring it on.' She saw Sarah blink in confusion, but she quickly recovered.

'Just watch, you smug bitch,' Sarah said and tore her clothes off. 'You'll beg me to kill you.' She slapped shampoo on Raina's head and squirted liquid soap on her body. With a sponge, she rubbed her skin. Raina's wounds burnt and a bloodcurdling scream escaped her unsteady throat when Sarah cleaned her arms and wrists.

'That's nice and foamy!' Sarah said as loud as she could with one hand pressed over her wound and the other over the water knob. The hose released ice-cold water yet again and Raina shivered. Her body went numb once more and her ears throbbed with a sharp pain travelling into her skull. She couldn't hear anything for some time, before her ears tuned back in. Her headache spiked up. She could barely stand against the wooden top.

'Oh look, you aren't funny anymore,' Sarah said and rubbed her skin once again to dry her. This time, Raina did not try to hold back. She screamed and cried as much as she could. Her wrists started to bleed again. Sarah snorted in disgust and cleaned it with some cotton and disinfectant before slapping on some ointment. She proceeded to wrap them in bandages, one by one.

'Once Hera is done, I'm going to repeat this routine as long as it takes for you to die, bitch. I'll splash you, I'll rub you, and put salt and lime juice on your cuts until your body peels off into nothing. What say?'

Raina gritted her clattering teeth and glared at her. That was all she could do, all she had been left capable of.

Next, Sarah made her wear a maroon corset and a maroon vintage ballroom dress with lace. The silk dress was immaculate. In any other situation, Raina would've felt like a royal. At that moment, though, she felt like a puppet whose strings were about to be cut off. Ved came back inside and moved Raina onto a chair. Sarah put make-up on her and did her hair in nineteenth-century ballroom fashion. She made her wear gaudy ballroom shoes and put on silk gloves to cover her arms.

'That will cover those hideous cuts and bandages nicely,' Sarah said, sounding pleased with her work.

'Can we transfer her to the studio?' Ved asked, so excited he almost glowed.

'Yes, take her.'

Ved yanked her up by an arm and twisted it behind her back. She screamed again.

'Be careful, don't make her cuts bleed before she is done with the shoot. And tears would ruin the make-up,' Sarah told him.

Ved loosened his grip, but not enough for her to wriggle out, in case there was any energy left in her to cause more trouble. Raina's stomach growled in hunger despite all the misfortune and torture. It amazed her how much hungrier she seemed to get with every passing minute, how much her body struggled to get out in one piece and return to normalcy despite what was happening.

It was shocking to her how strong her will to live was. *It is not new, though,* thought Raina. *This has happened before, worse than this. The only difference is that I may not live through this ordeal ...* Ved pushed the door of a room across the torture chamber. They entered a clean space, with beautiful wallpaper. The room was brightly lit with LED lights in a studio setup. He made her sit on an ornate wooden chair and tied her ankles to a set of chains fixed to the floor. Something like a handcuff clicked shut at her feet. He then covered up the chains under the flare of her skirt. *Danse Macabre* played again, and Ved answered at once.

'She's ready, Mother. Okay, I'll go up and keep an eye on him .... The swan boy is still leaking. What should I do once he's empty? I'll ... what? Oh, okay, I'll dump the body if it's not up to your taste. I'll get to work right away.' He put his phone back in his pocket and looked at her coldly, 'You should be thankful she decided to make you a special case. Gives you a bit more time to live.'

Raina wanted to retort, but her headache was still bad. She could only clench her fist and watch him go. She let out a shuddering, resigned breath, and stared blankly at the wall in front of her. The swan boy must be the guy Hera was torturing back in her room.

What pleasure did it give Hera? she thought, wondering why people like to torture others. *And what pleasure did it give him when he* ... A small voice, that of a teenage girl, always screamed for answers. Raina had no answers for herself or for that young girl. Those stony hands would always choke her in her head, and those eyes of the man possessed by a demon would never stop glaring at her. They hadn't stopped when she was working; they didn't stop now when she was trapped in a basement.

Raina hadn't dated anyone for years after leaving her home. Whatever little dating she had done ended in a few weeks, before her boyfriend's hands could remind her of the cold, knotted fingers that had almost choked her. In the end, unfortunately, her fear did come true. The one person she had trusted, allowed herself to feel something for, had almost choked her with chloroform.

She blinked. Something was strange.

OEUVRE

Beyond the blinding lights, something caught her eye. She stared at the wall where hung many big, gilded frames showcasing paintings. But these were not the usual paintings that one sees. These were bizarre pictures; pictures of men and women with strange faces. She watched one of them carefully, and her eyes widened with a horrifying realisation.

In the brightly lit underground room, the walls and ceiling were the same cream colour. The ceiling was adorned with an extravagant chandelier. The room had display lights at perfect angles above each frame, like in museums or art galleries. Raina felt like she was at an artist's exhibition. The photograph in front of her, the biggest on the wall, was of none other than Hera's dead husband. However, his face was not the handsome or lively one that she had seen in the news articles.

The left side of his face was skinned, and the eyelid had been removed. His hair was swept back neatly, and he was dressed in a white robe, similar to a Greek toga.

A golden crown sat on his head. In his left hand was a bouquet of red roses. In his right hand, he held a spear shaped like a lightning bolt but with its tip bent like a limp fish. What made her skin crawl was a patch of skin on the left side of his chest, showing from the himation draped over his left arm. The stitches on the chest were done with a black thread. He was clearly dead, sitting right where she sat now.

Her eyes wandered to the other paintings. The more carefully she looked, the more alarmed she got. A little away was a photo of a dead woman with her eyelids stitched to her eyebrows, staring fixedly at the opposite wall, with hands holding her own heart: the real organ. Another man was patched up with what looked like plucked chicken skin sewn on his body with colourful threads. His lips were painted red and his eyelids were smeared with black kohl. Many men and women stared at each other, their cloudy eyes covered with contact lenses, skins stitched and patched, dressed in different costumes and caked with make-up. Bile rose in her throat as she realized that the red paint used to paint these corpses before the photoshoot most likely was blood.

'Appreciating my art?' a voice boomed.

Raina gasped and whipped her head towards the door. Hera stood there with an enigmatic smile on her face. 'This is my studio. I take my pictures here. Sometimes, I even paint here. What do you think of it?' she asked, moving towards Raina.

'I think it is disgusting,' Raina retorted, bitterness rife in her voice.

'That's heartbreaking. But then, you have no sense of art,' Hera said with a chuckle. Her finger caressed the gilded frame of her husband's picture. 'A himation was worn by the ancient Greeks—'

'I don't need to hear any of this,' Raina said.

'—Where they draped it over their left shoulder, not right, like in the picture of my dear late husband. Can you understand why it's the opposite for him?'

'Fuck you,' Raina hissed.

'It's because the human heart is on the left side, and his heart was rotten. I wanted to show his real face, the ugliness and deceit behind his charming smile that people loved, so I skinned his left side. I patched the skin of the whore he had been seeing over his heart. The robe was draped over his right shoulder to show that fact. It's symbolic,' Hera concluded with nonchalance.

'Stop,' Raina was shaking now. Hera exuded a coldness that was far more unnerving than the icy water that had been repeatedly splashed on her.

'Look here,' Hera said excitedly. 'The lightning he wields is going limp as well. His ego, ideology and mind were all suffering from gangrene. Oh, and he could never get it up with me after a point. In the next frame you see a woman holding her own heart—' Hera pointed towards the next morbid picture. 'She was a production manager back in the day who did not obey me. One day, her arrogance crossed a line, and it made me want to put her in my collection. She didn't have respect for me in her heart. Isn't it cool I made her hold it out for me?' Hera smiled beatifically. 'This man with the chicken skin?' she continued. 'He had one task, just one thing to do. Slip poison into his artist's drink, just to make her sick and abandon a show. Not to kill her or anything, and yet, he didn't do it out of fear of being caught. Cowards deserve to be called chicken. And then this picture ... you already know the story of this one, don't you?' Hera said, looking at Raina with wide eyes.

Raina peered at the wooden frame. When she saw the picture, her lungs shrunk in terror.

'It's Savos!' Hera said gleefully. 'I covered half his face with rat skin and put patches of his whore on his chest. The tattoos are rat blood. Ahhh ... he was a difficult one, for I had to wear a mask while I did him. Rat blood can be infectious, Don cautioned me,' she said and turned to look at Raina. Her composure seemed to ebb away. 'You hurt Don badly. You will pay for it all,' she said, a vein in her forehead throbbing. 'You will pay by being the only one to have a before and an after.'

'Wh-what do you mean?' Raina stuttered slightly, her voice scarcely escaping her throat.

'Oh, Raina, Raina, Raina ...' Hera came closer. The only sounds were of Raina's chains clicking as her legs shook. 'You have caused me a lot of trouble and humiliation. I have to make you pay for it, you understand?' Hera's lips parted into a wide grin, and her eyes grew bright. 'This is my body of work, right here in this room, my *oeuvre*!

You will decorate the empty corner of my wall here, next to Savos.

'Say … Should I patch Ronit's skin over your heart as well? But wait, you don't know yet. He betrayed you.'

'What did you do to him?' Raina asked, more so to confirm the feeling of foreboding she had since he knocked her out. 'You must have blackmailed him to—'

'I told him to get closer to you, and he did, a few months ago. I told him to come back here today to get you out of your hiding hole, and he did. I told him to help me capture you and he did. You know what else he did for me? He came up with the perfect plan to get you, here in the first place,' Hera said.

'No,' Raina said, tears filling up her eyes.

'Oh, my dear.' Hera took the edge of her nightgown and wiped her tears. Raina's heart stopped for a second in an inexplicable fear. This woman's influence extended far beyond what she had imagined.

'You were trying too hard, harder than anyone in the past, to destroy me. I needed to keep a close watch on you. Ronit owed me, and I knew I could trust him. I wanted you here tonight to change your mind, to throw you off my scent. But it did not go as I had wanted, sadly, because you didn't leave with him. You stayed, and you poked that big, pointy nose around. I had to keep you here for the night and be good to you. My intentions were all favourable. But you had to flutter about. If only you had shut up and stayed inside the room, everything would've been fine. I'd have *Glitterbug* own up to its mistakes. But you had to ruin it all.'

'What was Ronit's part in this plan?' Raina asked.

'I think you know,' said Hera with a smirk.

Raina stared at Hera. That porcelain face of hers was perfect, inhuman.

'Did he fish the invite out from the garbage can and tell Vin?'

'Of course he did. He had to get you here, or I'd have had his name dropped from the directorial debut shortlist. In fact, he came to me with this plan. I invited you because Ronit suggested it would work.'

Raina's lips quivered and fresh tears formed in the corner of her eyes. She had been traded for a directorial debut, something Ronit could have easily achieved, sooner or later, with his skills and network.

Hera seemed to read her mind. 'This is what men do, Raina,' Hera said, wiping her tears gently with her gown. 'They betray. And because they betray, I had to wield power over them. Making them fear me is the only way to survive. Men worship what they fear. Only if I am worshipped can I be free of their binds. Whether it's a father, a husband, a son or a lover, if I want them to be loyal to me, I have to get them to worship me. If you had used his feelings to your advantage, like I used his ambition for my goal, you wouldn't be here.'

'You are twisted.'

'So is the world, good morning!' Hera waved a hand in her face, as if to wake her up. 'But you should know.

You, of all people, should know. We are so similar and yet you act like you do not understand me.'

'No! We are not similar. You have killed everyone who crossed you.'

'Why, isn't that what you do if you want it your way?' Hera snorted. 'Anyway, everyone I killed did not make it to this room.' She waved a hand at the walls, and her eyes sparkled. 'This room shows how I got where I am today, and where I will be in the next decade or so ... And you get to be a part of it. You should be honoured, Raina!'

'This is insane! Let me go!' Raina shouted through her headache. Hera's smile turned into a grimace. Her nose flared as she exhaled furiously.

'Do not destroy my frame with that crying. It's too late for any kind of a deal and my interest in you has waned. You are not as special as I thought. Stop whining and accept your fate,' she stated and turned towards the door.

On the side of the door, in a small corner, was a tripod stand fitted with a DSLR. Hera picked it up and checked the settings while positioning it in front of Raina. She shut the door behind her and switched a few lights off. The spotlight focused on Raina's face the most.

'This will come out beautifully ... I want you to think of ... your daddy.'

Raina flinched and looked at Hera, who was leaning over the stand to set up the angle for her shot.

'Look into the camera, Raina, and think of your daddy. Think of the lens as his eyes. Think of how his presence felt. Didn't he love you like a princess?'

'What do you know about him?' Raina whispered.

'He loved you as much as my daddy loved me, isn't that right?' Hera chuckled, enjoying every bit of the flavour in Raina's scared face. 'Look into your daddy's eyes, Raina, right here in the camera.'

The smell of alcohol mixed with blood filled her nostrils. She could feel one cold hand on her shoulder while the other slithered around her neck. She could hear his ghost whispers. His chiselled face with murderous eyes was looking at her, blood gushing down his head. The sound his footsteps made when he wore his brown leather shoes worsened her headache. That vibrating sensation and creaking bed, his eyes rolling up with heavy moans, and then a loud crash. It was all in her mind. It had to be!

A gunshot came from above their heads and echoed throughout the house. Hera frowned and opened the door to listen closely. Across the studio in the torture chamber, Sarah had stopped what she was doing and was looking up at the basement exit. She called out to Ved, but he didn't answer.

'He always answers,' she said to Hera, trying to call again.

'Sarah, go check,' Hera said. Sarah jogged out of the basement immediately.

Of what Raina could pick up from their activities, she knew this distraction was her only chance. While Hera looked worried for her son, watching the basement gate and turned away from her, Raina thought hard—and got an answer.

Something hot surged inside Raina's veins. A blinding, almost demonic presence took possession of her body. She got up, pushing the wooden chair back, and grabbed the tripod stand in front of her. Before Hera could realize what was happening, Raina swung it like a sword and smashed it into Hera's skull. She went down like a ton of bricks, half her body out of the door.

'Come on!' Raina pulled at the chains nailed to the floor but to no avail. She didn't have much time and had to figure out a way. The keys! Hera would have had the keys.

She grabbed Hera's ankles and pulled her closer to search her pockets. Nothing but a gun came out. She looked into the bullet chamber. Six bullets were ready to be shot with loud bangs which would warn all the crazies in the house. But what the hell! She would be free before they rushed back. So, Raina shot two bullets—one at the last link of each chain—and prepared to run.

She heard Hera grunt, trying to get up, and that made her speed up her departure, ignoring her wounds, aches and hunger. Raina groaned through her sealed lips as her body screamed and climbed up the wooden stairs stained with blood and dotted with pieces of flesh. She opened the door and a gush of fresh air flowed over her face, washing away the stale basement air and the stink of blood.

—

Fifteen minutes before the gunshot broke the dead silence of Hera's mansion, Ved had opened the door to his room on the first floor, opposite Hera's room. It was dark inside. He switched on the dim interior lights. Ved's room had black walls with silver grunge textures. The floor was white and glossy, reflecting the dim lights. A cowering Ronit was seated on a black leather couch, holding his head with both hands and shaking in the dreadful silence. It was past four in the morning, and the sky was at its darkest. He was wondering what he had got himself into just to accelerate a career already on the upswing.

'Come, help me dump the swan. It's lying in my mother's room,' Ved commanded.

'I didn't sign up for this.'

'It's not a request. Do as I say. We need to bury the body before dawn.'

Ronit finally raised his head. As he looked into Ved's baleful eyes, he realized he wouldn't win with words. He tried anyway.

'The plan was to make her compliant, not kill her,' he said.

'The plan didn't work because you fucked up. If she meant so much to you, you should've got her to quit and taken her with you,' Ved snarled. 'Now get up or I'll fill you with lead.'

Ved pointed his gun at him. Without a choice, Ronit got up and followed him. They reached Hera's room, and the sight that greeted them made him nauseous. The boy sprawled over the white floor had been stabbed a dozen times in the chest by what looked like a big, metal hairpin.

'His whining pissed Mother off and he got the punishment,' Ved said, very matter of fact. 'Grab his arms.'

Ronit couldn't move. His blood had turned cold. What started as just a small favour, just a little nudge into the grey area, had spiralled out of his control. Had he known things would come to this he would never have got involved with these psychopaths. But he'd been blinded by the promise of a directorial debut ... How could he have known? It all seemed so frivolous now. His vision blurred.

'I can't—I can't touch it,' he said in a shaking voice. 'It's a corpse.'

'Do it now!' Ved screamed and punched Ronit in the jaw. He somehow managed not to fall by steadying himself along the edge of Hera's bed. Heart racing and head floating, he positioned himself to hold the dead man's arms. Ved was already gripping the ankles. As he grabbed the limp, lifeless arms, his fingers felt wet and slippery. Something squelched. Blood and flesh.

'I can't do this,' he muttered, staring at the young man's face that was growing increasingly hazy for him. The boy was barely twenty years old. He probably hadn't grown a full beard yet. 'I won't ... '

'What the fuck are you waiting for? Pick his arms—'

The sentence was never finished as Ved fell back. A flying metal point struck him squarely under his left brow, missing his eye by millimetres. Ronit rushed towards the door. Ved screamed in agony and pulled out his gun, rolling to his stomach. With one good eye, he aimed and shot right in the back of Ronit's head. More blood and flesh fell on the floor. Ronit dropped right before the door he was dashing towards, missing his opportunity to escape by a second.

Ved writhed on the floor and cursed. It was the worst day of his life, the unluckiest night. And it was all because of one woman. Raina was the bearer of curses and ill-will, he was convinced. Her entry into their lives had caused a ruckus, and her presence had beckoned a destructive hurricane.

Ever since she had written the article, Hera's mood had been unpredictable. Ved had to get more bodies. It had been a tough few months dealing with Hera's grumpy mood, and it was all because of that cursed girl.

'I'll torture her so, so long!' he growled. Strobes of pain shot from his left eye and spread across his brain, making him twitch and sweat.

'Ved!' Sarah came running and fell beside him on her knees. She pressed a handkerchief over his wound.

'I'll kill that bitch! That cursed bitch!' he growled like a mad dog. Sarah put her arm below his neck to lift him up.

'It's thankfully not deep. Just keep the pressure on it. The doctor is on his way.'

'He's still an hour away,' Ved said as he stifled a cry. Waves of pain washed over him, turning his face red. 'It's okay. You should go to Mother. I have a bad feeling about it all.'

As if he had spoken the words of Nostradamus, two

gunshots echoed below them. Colour faded from their face. Sarah called Hera twice, but there was no answer.

'Go, get Mother out safely. I'll follow. And Sarah, if you spot her, kill her,' Ved said. He looked at Sarah gravely with the one good eye. She hesitated for a few seconds, but finally nodded and left.

Sarah was raging as she ran out. She took another staircase near Hera's room—a smaller, wooden one that flanked the fireplace. Raina hadn't noticed it, as it was in an alcove beside the huge hearth. Sarah went downstairs quietly, like a cat, and hid behind a wall a few steps away. This wall separated Hera's staircase and the area towards the kitchen. A small space behind the staircase was the secret gateway to the basement. Sarah stood there, waiting. Any moment now Raina would stumble out of the hidden door which was disguised as a wall. So she stared at the approximate point where the door was. The narrow space between the secret staircase and the basement door left no room to run or hide. A potted palm stood near the staircase to disguise the narrow space. She would shoot Raina right in her head the moment she came out, Sarah decided.

—

Not only was Raina's back killing her, but she was also not sure who lay in wait on the other side of the door. The gunshots would have alerted her hunters. Her brain burnt the remaining surge of energy thinking about her next steps as she toiled up the wooden stairs—and came up with a strategy. She got on all fours, hiding behind the last two steps, as she slowly opened the gate, and first pushed out the tripod stand she had held on to, out through the crack in the door. A bullet came smashing on the top and the stand fell from her hand, crashing down the basement stairs.

'Got you ...' Raina said and raised the gun she had taken from Hera. 'Four bullets left,' she whispered to herself, watching Sarah walk towards her from the crack in the door, and swung open the gate.

Sarah was walking towards her to confirm the hit. For a moment, just as Sarah came into view, their eyes met. Raina pulled the trigger. A bullet struck a hole in the wall beside Sarah. Before Sarah could take a shot, Raina put her full weight into a forward thrust and charged into her like a bull, screaming. Sarah fell back, firing at the ceiling. The gun fell from her hand.

However, Sarah wasn't defeated just yet. She flipped Raina over expertly, and put an arm around her neck in a chokehold, pinning Raina against her clavicle. Raina struggled and tried to instinctively claw Sarah's arm away—a mistake. The gun fell from Raina's hand. She kicked her legs and managed to push Sarah back against the palm plant, but nothing she did loosened Sarah's hold on her neck. Her eyes were beginning to bulge. Soon she would choke into nothing. If only she had not missed her mark ...

As the thought of death floated in and out of her mind, she remembered the bullet wound in Sarah's neck.

'Die, bitch ...' Sarah's voice hissed into Raina's ear in pure rage. Sarah was tightening her grip, slowly choking the life out of Raina, when a sharp pain in her neck made her muscles go slack. Raina had managed to reach Sarah's neck, wriggled a finger into her bandage and stabbed her wound, nail first, digging deeper. Sarah screamed and tried to reach the gun Raina had let go of, but Raina probed deeper with her finger—teeth gritted in disgust, fear and will to survive—and hooked her finger to yank out a chunk of flesh. Hot blood gushed out of the fresh wound and Sarah screamed in agony. It was enough time for Raina to reach for the gun that had slipped from her hand and point it at Sarah's face.

Sarah glared at Raina, heaving and groaning in pain as life ebbed away from her veins.

'You won't escape,' she said menacingly.

'Neither will you,' Raina said and shot her in the head.

Even the bullet hadn't managed to make Sarah flinch. In the last moments of her life, all she had was bitterness and rage in her eyes. Raina coughed deeply, her eyes tearing up again, and massaged her neck. Sarah was lying on the floor, still scowling at her. She didn't seem dead even as blood trickled down the hole in her forehead and pooled under her back on the floor.

Raina felt faint. Sick. It was just like the scene she had witnessed long ago and had been trying to forget ever since. She swayed on the spot and leaned over the palm plant, tearing some leaves as she clutched it. Her throat was sore and dry like wood.

The kitchen ... she thought.

It wasn't far away. She remembered that while covering the tour, the kitchen had a vegetable patch with shrubbery and some trees lining a wooden picket fence facing a road. If Hera's kitchen had the same layout, she could break a board or two with a brick. She wouldn't have to run through the muddy, grassy estate or shoot hounds! On the other hand, she could run only as fast as her beaten body would allow on a road.

Raina was about to turn when she remembered her phone was in Sarah's pocket. She bent to pick up her phone and also the gun Sarah had been using. There were five bullets left in Sarah's gun, three in her own, and her phone was still thirty per cent alive. Enough to get a cab out of this place. She would head straight to the Mumbai Police.

She wedged the phone between her corset-wrapped breasts and dragged herself towards the kitchen, two guns in her hands.

—

Hera stared at her palms. They were covered in blood. She could feel a trickle run down the back of her head and soak into the silk of her robe. She had never experienced such physical pain before. Just thinking about how much more pain her victims would have felt with every stab, cut and bullet wound excited her. Knowing that she had made them feel pain worse than this was almost orgasmic.

However, she also felt displeased. Raina had knocked her out for precious minutes.

'Unforgivable ... just when I think she has lost ...'

Yet another gunshot had sent Ved spiralling into rage. He turned over on his side and got up while still trying to press his wound close. His gut was uneasy, and his heart thrummed rapidly. He felt an uneasy sense of foreboding; he had been this way ever since Raina had entered their lives. He rummaged through Hera's cupboards till he found a first-aid kit. After administering some basic care to his eye, he gulped down a handful of aspirins and tried to control his uneven breathing.

'Sarah ... Sarah ... Sarah ...' he muttered, pressing his wound.

PANDEMONIUM

Hera couldn't believe her eyes. She had stumbled over Sarah's lifeless body, and now she stood shaking in rage. She looked into the glazed eyes, still intense and sharp after death, as she stepped back from the pool of blood. She had to blink twice to clear the view; her head was a pit of burning agony, her vision slightly blurry. Blood trickled into her silk gown carving a path on her neck somewhere behind her tangled hair.

As she stared at Sarah, she swayed in a hypnotic wave. Heat rose from her skin under the smooth fabric. Sarah had never missed her target. Not once. She had been a cold assassin since her first job. Yet, after killing over a hundred people, this is how she met her end. She lay in her own blood with a bullet in her head and a gaping hole in her neck.

She might have been her stepdaughter, but Hera had liked her.

'I will see her dead,' Hera resolved, fingers curling around the trigger of a Combat Master she had taken from her studio. The thought of a 9 mm bullet drilling into Raina's face formed a sneer on her ghastly porcelain face. She trudged towards the kitchen, following the faint footprints of blood on the white marble.

The house had filled up with a liquid light as the ambience of a clear dawn after a hellish monsoon night hit the misty air. An absolute silence had fallen, as if the house were a trembling rabbit hiding from a hunter.

'You cannot run forever, little bug. I'm coming to blast your head off!' she hissed and chuckled.

Raina chugged some water from a jug. Cold water revitalized her cramping insides. She now needed to eat and sleep with aspirins and paracetamol in her system; she felt weak and feverish. The hot breath she exhaled and the dull ache in her head told her she was burning up. She was too tired to even lift her arms; her body felt a ton heavier than her sixty-kilo self.

A sharp pain shot across her lower back and she put her arms on the black stone surface of the kitchen island to support herself. Two arrows of pain shot through her flesh and bones from each of her wrists. She gritted her teeth to muffle the scream and lost her balance, falling. This time, she managed to prevent crashing nose first with her elbows and pushed herself up again.

'Shit,' she said, heaving and wincing with each inhale and exhale, resting her grip on the gun in her hand. It wouldn't be as easy to escape as she had imagined.

The kitchen was big. A long kitchen island divided the white space with steel storage units alongside the wall beside a steel double door. A minimalistic, L-shaped black marble top was fitted with multiple stoves and sinks. Shiny utensils hung from hooks, motionless and silent as if trying to hide in plain sight. A weak light made the steely residents glimmer as if they had eyes of rabbits peeking from underground holes, sniffing trouble.

Run ... Cannot run ... life runs out ...

Breathing rapidly, Raina swept her gaze across the kitchen counter. The door at the far right led to the vegetable garden outside. Two windows flanking the door were shut closed, but light seeped through the gaps between the panes and hinges. She realized that the sun was rising. Finally, it was time to end this nightmare ... but the door to her freedom was shut closed with a heavy-duty sliding bolt in the middle and a thick vertical bolt at the top with a hydraulic hinge system that did not need a lock.

She motivated herself to get up and make a run for it. Going to her rented shithole—that now appeared to be heaven in comparison to this hell—to pack up her stuff was a necessary risk, but what after that ...? She would plan all that later, once she was safe. Beyond the gate lay the road that would lead her straight out of the cursed estate and away from the crazies of the house—

CLANK!

The kitchen door where she had come in from hit against the wall. Raina froze.

'There you are, bitch,' Hera said. Her maddened stare

fell on Raina, who was sitting in plain sight against the side edge of the kitchen island.

Before Raina could move her body or even gasp, Hera's 9 mm was rocketing towards her. Without thinking, her body swayed away, and the grip over her gun tightened. Raina shot almost simultaneously. The 9 mm blasted through the outer layers of Raina's shoulder, scraping the bone. Raina's bullet hit Hera in her thigh, and she fell with a grunt, immediately taking cover behind the kitchen island. On the other side of the same kitchen island, Raina screamed, clutching her left shoulder, trying to blink tears away. The nightmare seemed to be unending. Why the hell could she not escape?

'If you shoot again, I'll get your brains next,' Raina said in a low voice—the voice of a person barely holding onto sanity.

At this point, she was so furious that she wanted to burst Hera's eyes with her thumbs. A sudden anger, an urge to fight instead of running away, flared up. It pumped her body with adrenaline. Her head cleared up and her senses sharpened. The sleeves of her ballroom gown were soaked in blood that was dripping onto the floor from the cuffs. Raina ignored her pain as her anger turned into fury.

'That's more like it. You sound more like yourself now, don't you?' Hera said in a shaky voice and sneered despite the cold sweat enveloping her like a shroud.

Blood flowed through her fingers alarmingly fast even as she clutched her thigh. 'You want to kill me more than I want to kill you.'

'And whose fault is that?' Raina snapped.

She tore the cloth of her skirt lining and wrapped it around her shoulder, holding a corner with her teeth. Hera, meanwhile, had taken the belt out of her silken robe and was trying to tie it around her wound, but the bleeding wouldn't stop. Her femoral vein was spared, but that made it no less dangerous.

An agonized scream echoed through the house. Ved had finally discovered his beloved's dead body and was wailing. He screamed and cried. Raina felt a strange satisfaction listening to him. She wondered why but she knew the answer somewhere deep inside; she couldn't stand to see the love they had. Maybe, that was the real reason why she had shot Sarah in the head.

A few seconds later, suddenly silence fell; an ominous silence. Hera sat quietly. Raina shifted slowly towards the edge, trying to calculate her moves.

'I will kill her!' Ved announced loud enough for the world to hear, 'I will bring you her blood!'

As Ved's wrath echoed in the house, Raina urged her body to move, any sense of evil satisfaction gone after Ved's declaration.

'You asked whose fault it was,' Hera continued as if nothing had interrupted them, her voice cold. 'What do you think? Is it your fault that you kept digging with the intention to destroy me? Or is it my fault to think you were special enough to be persuaded?'

'Have you finally lost it?' Raina said, irascible.

'I knew it ... it is your fault. You never gave it a thought. But then again, a snake is born with its poison; why rebuke it for trying to bite?'

Raina opened her mouth to retort but thought better of it. On her phone was the evidence of Don killing Savos. There was evidence of Hera indulging in perverse sexual activities. She could escape with it ... but nowhere did the evidence record things Hera had said or done that night outside her room. If not crush Hera's eyes with her thumbs, she could at least get solid evidence against her.

She fished out the phone resting in her corset slowly with her right hand while still holding onto the gun. The left arm was limp at her side, throbbing in pain. Blood smeared on the glass screen as she unlocked her phone and started to record.

'Hera, do you even understand what you are saying? You sound drunk and useless.'

'On the contrary, I feel as clear as I ever have,' Hera replied coolly. 'Raina, we were born of poison, and that's why we became like we are,' Hera said, strangely calm.

Her eyes glinted in a thought distant from where she was.

'You want to blame your father for letting Balram exploit you? That's exactly what you do to young artists. You made them carry out your crazy fantasies. You even killed the guy from yesterday's party!' Raina egged her on. 'What was he, twenty?'

'My father didn't just get me to sleep with him!'

Hera's voice flared. 'He made a minor sleep with a man against her will! He bartered me to repay his debt. And no one helped me, not even mom. Of course, I want to punish the world for it,' Hera said, stressing every word. 'I had to make my dad and my rapist learn a lesson. So, I killed them. And I will make the world bow down to me, worship me. That's why I made them suffer like I did.'

'But you killed other people too!' Raina said. 'You didn't have to do that.'

'Killing one is justified and killing more is a crime?' Hera said with a chuckle. 'I already had murder on my hands; one or two or fifty, that's not the problem here. You should understand something. After you kill once, you can't stop. Sometimes you have to kill to cover up your tracks, and sometimes ... well, sometimes it's just convenient. Even fun. The boy upstairs started whining. I skewered him with my hairpin. Can you imagine the pent-up anger I hold? Your existence only pushes me more!'

'This makes no sense. You didn't have to—'

'Shh! Listen to Ved,' she said suddenly.

Ved's cries had turned to war cries. He was shooting randomly, breaking down his own house to bits. He was smashing things and screaming for Raina to come out and face him.

'That's what happens when you lose someone who loved you. Revenge, madness and total loss of self-control. And this—' she pointed at herself, 'Hera ... Hera happens when your loved ones screw you up. Who do you focus your rage on? Who do you avenge? Who do you target? What good is your revenge? There is nothing left.

'You start to see the world from your distorted perspective. Betrayed and chained in her home, Hera has to hit back in some way. Hera has to invoke fear to be worshipped and to right the wrongs done to her. People call her jealous, brutal and unfeeling, but is that the truth? Is the truth that simple? People never look into their own hearts. They see what their mind allows them to see,' Hera rambled on, looking distantly at the ceiling, turning paler as the blood flowed fast from her leg. 'Disillusioned, looking through their filthy glasses, they think the stains are on the others.

'Never me, always you, when high tide comes;

'Never you, always me, when the tide turns ...'

The recording counted from seconds to minutes. Raina stayed still and silent. There was something true and discomforting about Hera's words.

'For instance, you, Raina. You hate me not because I have murdered other people or tortured young artists. You hate me because I became Hera and you couldn't,' Hera said, smirking.

'Wh-what?' Raina breathed in.

'While you dug up dirt on me, did you really think I didn't dig up anything on you?' Hera said as calmly as ever. Raina's throat was a lump of dried meat.

'Your father didn't die of a tragic accident. You pushed him down the stairs,' Hera said with a laugh.

BAD BLOOD

It was a clear morning. The hot sun had risen amidst humid winds rushing into Mumbai from the sea. A clay wind-chime clinked pleasantly somewhere downstairs. Raina's attention was focused on the sound of that chime. She had to focus on anything but her mind's agitation and her heart's crazy drumming. What happened the previous night was a real nightmare. Her father—the man who had taught her to walk, who had played with her in parks when she was little—had violated her. Her world was falling apart, moorings cut cruelly. There was pain, there was numbness, there was a yawning abyss in her heart she didn't know how to close.

There was not one person she could rely on. Loneliness and fear had haunted her for more than a year now since her mother died. Was it not enough for him? Did he have to ruin her so completely?

Raina had had enough. It was time now, time to end it all. She had thought long and hard about it and had come up with a plan. Things were perfectly aligned that day, as if fate supported her decision. Her father was starting a new job and had ordered her to carry his lunch downstairs to his bike. Instead of going down, she waited in front of the stairs, just outside the door with a big steel lunchbox in her hand. She looked at her neighbour's door. A big lock hanging at the outer door confirmed that the family next door had already left for work. On Mondays, better arrive earlier than your boss! That's what her father wanted to do to make a good first impression. With his anger management issues, she wondered how he had got another job. Did he play a depressed widower? Or was a bad temper not an issue for a shipping yard manager? But that was not the question that preoccupied her that morning.

All that mattered was that no one saw her standing there. It was seven, and everyone had their own offices to rush to. The opposite building hardly had a view of her. From the road outside, no one could see her. She repeated all of these points to herself over and over. As the wind picked up and the chimes made a low clink, she went through every step in her mind for the final time.

'Why the fuck are you standing here?' Her father stepped outside and shut the door behind him. She noticed the shiny brown leather shoes he was wearing.

'I'll walk with you as it's your first day,' she said. He pushed her chest against the wall with one hand, a laptop bag swaying in other.

'You are a whore-child. Don't try to act like a daughter to me,' he growled at her face, spraying her with fine spittle. He smelled good even in that mad anger. She observed how his scowl couldn't ruin his handsome face. And those cold, granite-black eyes ... they were alluring. In that moment, with her mind made up, she could even notice the details of the whorls in his beard and the fine olive tone of his skin with a tint of brown, instead of going all numb and blurry-eyed. 'I'll have you good tonight,' he said and pushed her hard again.

She winced but didn't avert her gaze. He turned towards the stairs. She followed. He took one step down, and Raina swung the steel lunchbox in her hand in a trance-like fury. It hit the side of his head hard. He lost his balance and fell head first. With every tumble, he hit his head.

Blood spurted out of his mouth and skull, leaving smears of red on his way down. At last, his body came to rest after bumping off the last stair. The man lay coughing blood and looked up at Raina with the same stony eyes. A single crease formed between his brows to show anger and pain together. His eyes stared at her, shocked that a little girl he had under his thumb could kill him. Raina stared back at him, without any regret.

The tinkle of the chimes and the wind rustling her hair were clear. She was present in that moment, more full of life than ever. It was only when a woman from downstairs screamed at the top of her lungs that she quietly stepped inside the house to wipe the blood off the lunchbox over a washbasin. She had packed decorative rocks from a pot inside her room in that lunchbox, not food.

She had to go outside and pretend to cry and break down; be the pitiful young girl of nothing but eighteen and a few months old who had been orphaned in a cruel twist of fate. She had to make sure they believed her tears.

And they did.

A policeman even offered her a handkerchief as he sat beside her, placating her with his wide palms rubbing her back, his leg touching hers. As she sobbed, he said he sympathized with her. His real interest lay in the view beyond the neck of her top. Raina let him sympathize, stare and rub her back.

Things went awry only when she realized how she had underestimated the guard in the opposite building.

'I know ...' Hera's voice sounded almost excited. 'I know what you did because someone told me. Guess who?'

No way, Raina thought. I destroyed the evidence and the ... and the witness.

'You're probably wondering how I know, or even how much I know,' Hera laughed and continued, 'Let me make things easy for you. After crushing your father's head, you succeeded in playing the pitiful orphan, but you couldn't stop the police investigation. They started questioning the guard who was on duty in the opposite building that day. A sixty-year-old man who had a family, a life, wouldn't you say? Unfortunately for him, he witnessed something he shouldn't have. His shift would start from seven every morning. The first thing he did every day was switch on the water pump on the terrace of the building. That day, too, he was coming down the stairs when he saw your dad manhandling you. Then he saw you murder him,' said Hera, really enjoying herself.

Raina couldn't move.

'You realized something was fishy when the police took him twice for questioning. The poor man did not reveal anything—you knew, didn't you? But he could break under pressure someday. You wouldn't risk that. So, you decided that any evidence and witness should be taken care of. You kept an eye on him, and one day, the opportunity presented itself. The guard had to cover a night shift in his colleague's place. What you did next was masterful; I'd have done the same! You crept inside the building by climbing a tree and walking over the boundary wall of the compound—of course, I wasn't there, but this is what I imagine you did—and in the deepest of the dark, you took out the bulbs in the vicinity, just like you broke my cameras. Then you crept into the poor guy's quarters. He had a little stove and cylinder there, for night duties.' Hera broke into laughter.

'Poor old man, he must've been out of it after the double shift. You loosened the cylinder plug, waited just long enough and threw in a lighter! He went pop like popcorn! Police concluded it was a gas leak that caused it. He smoked beedis, and it was usual for him to have a lighter or two.

I guessed it all. Tell me, isn't that accurate? The fire also destroyed any evidence he might have hidden, including the memory cards containing the CCTV footage from the day of your father's murder.' Hera laughed again and this time gasped for breath. Her vision was blurring. The blood loss made her feel faint.

Raina was too shocked to say or feel anything anymore. The secrets that she had kept hidden even from herself were tumbling out. Tears kept rolling down from her eyes uncontrollably.

'You know how I got all this? The old man wasn't the only one who saw you kill your father,' Hera said with a sly smile. Shock rattled Raina's spine. 'Back to the day you bid your daddy goodbye, the other guard, whose shift the old man had taken over, was upstairs helping with the pump. Unfortunately for you, they were both together. They both witnessed it. One of them, the younger one, got scared and didn't want any involvement with the police.

'To escape that, he ran back to his village. But he managed to take the footage with him—the footage you failed to burn—for leverage if it ever came to it. Do you know what's on that tape? Guess?' Raina's lips quivered.

'You're so clueless ... The old guy made a video on a cheap smartphone, first and foremost, to record your daddy's misbehaviour. He wanted to save you at that moment.'

'There was no video ...' Raina shook her head, more so to deny what she heard.

'But there was ... Why do you think he sealed his lips before the police?'

No answer.

'It was to save you ...'

Raina kept shaking her head, denying everything.

'Well ... it doesn't matter anymore. What matters is that after you pushed your daddy, the old man was shocked as hell. He decided never to show the video to anyone, so he handed the evidence to the other guard and asked him to hide it, in case they ever needed it. That was smart of him. The other guy took the phone back home.

'I got hold of the footage and his testimony on video for a big bag of cash. Anytime I need him to testify, he will, for more money. The old man was not so lucky. He stayed back and covered for his friend. He denied witnessing anything. He denied that the other guard was with him at all. But you know, the police can smell a fart in the air from miles. They continued questioning him. You got agitated. Maybe he would've succumbed to pressure one day? I guess we'll never know.' Hera's laugh was uncontrollable. She laughed as heartily as she could through the pain. Black spots had started dotting her vision.

'What's so funny?' Raina muttered.

'What's what?'

'What's so funny!' Raina screamed. The burning fury boiled her blood again. 'My father beat me, harassed me, almost raped me ... he killed my mother!' Tears streamed down her dark, grimacing face. 'Yes, I killed him. So what? He would've killed *me* otherwise. He was going to come back and ... and—'

'Liar!' Hera's voice echoed in the kitchen.

'You think I'd lie about what he did to me?'

'Liar! That's not why you killed him,' Hera shouted and thumped her fist on the microwave beside her. The kitchen island vibrated. 'Tell me the truth, Raina. Why'd you kill him?'

'He tried to rape me—'

'That's not why—'

'He was going to do it that night—'

'Not why—'

'He killed my mother—'

'Your mama's investment had fully matured and you had turned eighteen!' Hera screamed.

Silence fell black and heavy. They sat motionless, pressing their wounds and feeling the blood drip between their fingers. Ved's voice came from a distance. He was still shouting and rampaging outside in the garden where the barbeque grills had been.

'The day your mom died,' Hera continued, forcing Raina to confront the bitter truth, 'you could've told the police everything, but you stayed silent. You could've put him behind bars, but if you did that, your mother's investment money wouldn't go to you. He was her nominee. The whole sum would go to him. That's also why he killed your mother, by the way, so that he could claim it on maturity.

'When she died, the sum still had a full year left to mature. So you waited. Once your father had redeemed that amount, you let a few months pass, to avoid any suspicion. You turned eighteen and became, as an adult, the rightful heir of not only his bank account but also that wretched house.'

'That's not how it was,' Raina said, still shaking her head.

'Oh, come on, Raina. You planned it all from the very beginning. And it was brilliant too! You did well, enduring things up to a point and getting out of it without getting raped. But let's be honest, if he had tried to rape you before the amount was cashed in,' Hera paused to chuckle, 'you'd have let him.'

'I never planned any of it,' Raina hissed.

'Denial. You live in denial, Raina. That's why things went wrong for a brilliant woman like you. You deny yourself the obvious and easier path because you are unwilling to acknowledge the truth. There was no need for you to take up a shitty job, live a shitty life ... You could've lived comfortably with the money you got from his account and the sale of his house. But you let yourself be sucked into drudgery.

'You glorified your pain, played a victim in your own eyes and the world's, and suffered thinking you'd redeem yourself. Aren't I still going the right way?' Hera asked.

Raina didn't respond.

'I'll take that as a yes,' Hera said, undeterred. 'Now, tell me honestly, whose fault is it that we sit here, in this kitchen, bleeding and riddled with bullet wounds? Do you hate me or is it yourself you hate? Are the bloodstains only on my glasses or yours too?'

'No, I'm not like you,' Raina said, almost choking. Her heart was beating madly. 'You kill blindly, for sport. Anyone and everyone in your way is finished. You've tortured so many people, and you will never stop.'

'That's why you envy me,' Hera said. The mad grin on her face softened into a smile. 'You wanted to keep going after you felt the rush of getting your way, but you chickened out. If I were you, I'd have killed your boss a long, long time ago and taken the reins of the magazine into my hands. Run things like my racehorses. Made people dance like my whores. You hesitated!'

'You're mistaken,' said Raina. Her body shook as she took a deep breath in. 'I hate you because you torture and kill, and people never see that side of you. Even if you destroy them, they don't see it. I hate that you get your way because you are Hera. I hate that you don't need to do it, and yet, you choose to anyway.'

Hera's smile shrank. She frowned.

Raina continued. 'I hate that I had to bloody my hands to survive, but you didn't need to. You didn't have to be with the director after the first movie; it made you a star overnight. You didn't have to get your own manager to murder a Hollywood casting agent; you were already a supermodel! You didn't have to kill your husband; you could've simply divorced him for cheating on you—Sarah was the biggest evidence you had!

'You'd have got half his wealth lawfully. But no, you wanted more. And lastly,' Raina said, resting her head on the cold steel body of the kitchen island and gritting her teeth, 'you didn't have to cut up their corpses or defile their remains for your gory art!' Raina was finished.

The recorder ticking off more minutes was still recording.

'I don't expect the likes of you to understand my *oeuvre*,' Hera said, her body stiffening in anger. 'I was going to offer you to join me but not anymore. That stubborn head of yours ... it's no fun. I've decided you don't get to leave—alive or dead.'

'Why don't you try to stop me?' Raina had scooted to the edge of the kitchen island's base, inch by inch. It was clear from the direction of Hera's voice that she hadn't moved. Hera tried to shift, but a sharp pain rendered her leg useless. Only a few feet remained between Raina and the door ... but how would she buy time to open it?

Ved had searched most of the house. The cursed woman was not coming out. He was getting impatient with every bullet that he had to load after turning every door. As he stormed back into the hall, it clicked; he hadn't raided the kitchen yet. His lips pulled back into a wild sneer, and his brows squeezed in focus. He breathed deeply, as if trying to calm his nerves, and marched towards the kitchen door that stood wide open. With his heart beating madly as he approached his prey, he stepped closer, his ears attentive and feet quiet. Blood rushed to his head.

He had two long-barrelled guns full of magnum. His brain wasn't really functioning right anymore, and he was operating on pure adrenaline. All he knew was that he'd heard someone talk. He pointed both his guns at the first thing that came into view and began to shoot.

Hera screamed, moving against the storage units. Raina was at the edge of the kitchen island, ready to sprint, but had to take cover again. The magnums rained on the steel side, denting the tuff exteriors and ricocheting. Utensils clanked and fell at her feet. Ved roared along with his guns.

'Die for Sarah! Die for her, you cursed woman!' he howled. Bullet shells clinked on the floor. The barrage stopped for a split second. Before he could pull out another gun from his side holster, Raina stretched her arm and fired the remaining bullets from her gun randomly.

Ved crashed on the floor. Raina peeked from the edge and saw that the bullet had hit the side of his stomach.

'Ved!' Hera shrieked.

For the first time since she'd known her, Raina heard fear in her voice. Raina hoisted herself up and ran towards the door as fast as she could.

'No!' Hera screamed again. She shot at Raina, her eyes clouded over with rage. Raina escaped the aimless bullets and yanked the bolts open. She pushed the door ajar and ran outside into the vegetable garden like there was no tomorrow.

—

Hera hurried beside Ved despite her injuries and tried to stop the bleeding. However, Ved gripped her arm, grunting.

'It's okay, don't worry about me. Don't let her escape,' he said, his voice a hoarse whisper. 'I saw a phone in her hand when she ran. Get her. Please!'

Hera's face darkened. A phone? So that's why that sneaky bitch was talking so much, getting Hera to confess. She handed a kitchen cloth to Ved to stem his bleeding and held his hand.

'Hold on, no matter what,' she said. Ved gave a half nod his lips shut tightly to seal the pain in. Hera tightened the knot over her thigh and stood up. Holding on to the walls and edges, she walked outside.

Raina had made some headway, wading through the plants, shrubs and grass. The white picket fence surrounding the boundary resembled six-foot-high canines laid together side by side. There was no way to jump over them. There was a gate near a pumpkin patch, but it had a lock. Raina had no time to try to break it. So, she decided to unhinge the bolt instead. She picked up a rock and started to smash the barrel plate holding the bolt. Repeatedly, she raised it and crashed it, ignoring the exploding pain in her left shoulder. The wood attached to the plate was chipping and cracking, but it wasn't letting go. She saw Hera dragging her leg as she moved towards her.

'Come on,' she muttered to herself and crashed against the wooden boards harder. She could tell that it would soon give way and she would be free … almost. Mustering all her leftover energy, she pushed against the fence. The plate had almost come apart.

Run away … run forever …

Tip-tap-tip, her blood trickled as she forced the gate open.

'Stop, Raina, I still have some bullets left to blast your face off,' Hera shouted.

Her eyes appeared more insane in the sunlight. The bright morning rays, yellow gold, fell on her pale face and parched lips. Her bloodshot eyes were fixed on Raina. Hera slowly raised her arm and pointed a swaying gun at Raina.

'Come on!' Raina pleaded for the door to open and pushed it. Finally, the plate separated completely, and the gate sprang open. Hera saw her leap onto the road and was about to pull the trigger, but someone else was there.

'Wh … wait!' Raina screamed at the top of her lungs.

—

Hera removed her finger from the trigger and put the gun behind her back. A low rumble of an engine caught her by surprise. She shifted nearer to the open gate and saw Raina waving frantically. A yellow garbage truck pulled over close to her. There were two men inside. A burly young boy was peering from the passenger window beside another man who seemed to be around fifty.

They looked shocked to see a dishevelled woman dressed in a ballroom gown. Her sleeves and gloves had covered most of the cuts and bruises, and they couldn't guess how pale Raina looked behind the make-up that was still on.

However, humans can intrinsically sense danger, even if it is behind the tall grass or a wooden gate that seemed to have been broken out of. The men must have smelled blood because they asked Raina, 'Are you hurt somewhere, ma'am?' The young boy looked around, at the gate and back at her. So did the other man.

'Ma'am, are you all right? Do you need to call the police?' asked the older man, gripping the wheel tightly and looking at her.

Hera watched them even as waves of black splashed her eyes and her head floated. Cold sweat had drenched her. Yet, she stood listening, trying to stay awake. In her condition, she wouldn't be able to shoot all three of them. If the evidence got out ...

Raina's heart clamoured loudly, a thousand words storming her mind. She had escaped, and she had with her the evidence, shocking evidence that would bring an industry to a crashing halt.

There was bound to be an outcry when the industry's darling was exposed. There would be protests. There would be investigations, and there definitely would be people maligning her. A mob would possibly demolish Hera's studio, sets and offices; give the oppressed a reason to rage, and they will. She could end Hera once and for all.

Take me to the police. I have the evidence! I was right, and Vin was wrong! Ronit was wrong! Everyone who worships Hera is wrong! The world is wrong! She's got you fooled, weighed you down with cash! See it, realize it, do something about it!

Raina clutched hard at her phone. She stared harder at the duo. Her lips quivered. The skin on her back crawled. She felt Hera's hot stare, powerless to kill them all but determined to have revenge.

And then, tears rolled down her face. The grip on her phone relaxed, and she gasped. A thousand words choked her throat, stuck behind the one truth about herself she didn't want to expose.

'Drop me to the nearest cab, please ...' she said in a low, quaking voice. Hera blinked. 'I fell down some stairs after performing here in the event yesterday and got stranded ... I was left all alone.'

'Oh, dear, come sit inside. We'll drop you. This land surely is huge; even I get confused. Move, boy. Go to the back. Let her sit comfortably.'

The boy got out and held the door open for Raina. She took a heavy step towards the door. Before she could heave herself up into the truck's passenger seat, she turned to look at the gate she had broken. An outline of Hera in her black silk gown with one arm behind her back came into view. She was in the shadow of a tree. The men didn't notice her, but Raina knew she was there, watching them. Possibly grinning her mad grin.

She turned away from Hera and got into the truck. The boy shut the door for her and ran to the back. The man started the engine and put the truck in gear. She was driving away, but she wasn't happy.

'Are you sure you don't need more help?'

The man watched her with concern as he drove. Raina noticed the wrinkled skin on the man's face. His eyes were warm and full of life. A pincer cut at her insides. Raina's gaze dropped, and she looked away.

'I'm sure,' she squeaked, careful not to use her sleeves to wipe her tears lest the blood smeared her face. 'I should have left with my colleague when I could have, without getting lost.'

The man offered her a handkerchief and asked her to cheer up. She blotted her eyes on it, whispering her thanks.

The garbage truck ran smoothly on the long, black road leading out of the estate. Horses ran freely in the range spreading into the horizon beside her. They ran without halting, without heeding the mud spraying their prideful chests. Not the green grass nor the wind blowing after the rain made them stop.

They'll run and run … till life runs out of them. Yes, that is when they'll stop, when their feet no longer touch the ground.

ACKNOWLEDGEMENTS

> 'You can, you should, and if you're brave enough to start, you will.'
>
> – Stephen King, *On Writing: A Memoir of the Craft*

Even as one starts, a push is always helpful to keep the momentum going, especially for a writer. I am immensely grateful to Ravi Subramanian for giving my story a chance to be published in the series. Your support at every step has made this possible.

A big thanks to Vinita Nangia, the mind behind the *Times of India* Write India campaign, because of whom I met Ravi. It's a truly wonderful platform where aspiring authors can meet writers from all over the country. Being one of the top contestants of Write India was not only a boost to my confidence, but also the first step of my journey towards being a published author.

Sanghamitra, if a writer is the architect then an editor is the builder. Thanks for your inputs, corrections, discussions and all the support for every element of this book. Gavin, thank you for your patience and for creating a cover that is exceptional. What an exciting journey it has been!

Papa, thanks for being my inspiration for writing and for being my favourite storyteller. I write because you told me bedtime stories, because you printed out my first book when I was fourteen! You are not here to see me finally get published, but you knew I would get there, and every book I publish will be dedicated to you from my heart.

Last but not the least, to my family, friends, and especially my cousin Abhay who encouraged this procrastinating writer to complete my books and get them published. How could I have done this without you? I'm truly blessed to have you all in my life.

ABOUT THE AUTHOR

Ravi Subramanian is the award-winning author of ten novels. His stories are set against the backdrop of the financial services industry. He has won the Economist Crossword Book Award three years in a row, as well as the Golden Quill Readers' Choice Award. His books have been translated into Hindi, Tamil and Latvian. Visit him at www.subramanianravi.com or connect with him on Twitter @subramanianravi or on Instagram @Ravisubramanian70.

Mansi Babbar is a content creator and has her own podcast, Horror Originals. She was one of the top ten contestants in the *Times of India*—Write India campaign. Next to writing stories, she loves to binge watch shows on Netflix, camp out on starry nights and eat good food! You can reach her on www.mansibabbar.com or on her Instagram account @mansi_19.

30 Years *of*

HarperCollins *Publishers* India

At HarperCollins, we believe in telling the best stories and finding the widest possible readership for our books in every format possible. We started publishing 30 years ago; a great deal has changed since then, but what has remained constant is the passion with which our authors write their books, the love with which readers receive them, and the sheer joy and excitement that we as publishers feel in being a part of the publishing process.

Over the years, we've had the pleasure of publishing some of the finest writing from the subcontinent and around the world, and some of the biggest bestsellers in India's publishing history. Our books and authors have won a phenomenal range of awards, and we ourselves have been named Publisher of the Year the greatest number of times. But nothing has meant more to us than the fact that millions of people have read the books we published, and somewhere, a book of ours might have made a difference.

As we step into our fourth decade, we go back to that one word – a word which has been a driving force for us all these years.

Read.